Books are to be r
the last

D0716051

0 5 NOV 2004

0 5 JUN 2006

0 5 SEP 2007

0 5 JAN 2009

2 9 APR 2010

LIBREX —

ROUNDWOOD PARK SCHOOL

034780

By the same author

Blinded by the Light
Disconnected

SOMETHING WICKED

SHERRY**ASHWORTH**

Collins

An imprint of HarperCollins*Publishers*

ROUNDWOOD PARK SCHOOL
LIBRARY 034780

First published in Great Britain by HarperCollins*Children'sBooks* 2004
HarperCollins*Children'sBooks* is an imprint of
HarperCollins*Publishers* Ltd,
77-85 Fulham Palace Road, Hammersmith, London W6 8JB

The HarperCollins*Children'sBooks* website address is
www.harpercollinschildrensbooks.co.uk

1 3 5 7 9 8 6 4 2

Text copyright © Sherry Ashworth 2004

The author asserts the moral right
to be identified as the author of the work.

ISBN 0 00 712335 3

Printed and bound in England by
Clays Ltd, St Ives plc

Conditions of Sale
This book is sold subject to the condition
that it shall not, by way of trade or otherwise,
be lent, re-sold, hired out or otherwise circulated
without the publisher's prior written consent in any
form of binding or cover other than that in which
it is published and without a similar condition
including this condition being imposed
on the subsequent purchaser.

Thanks to Andy, Dave, Dominic, Jenny, Michael and all at Relaunch. And Robyn and Rachel, of course.

For Chris and Libby.

CHAPTER ONE

Everything keeps going round and round in my head, so it'll be a relief to tell you everything, just as it happened. Not because I want to claim I'm innocent – the opposite, in fact. I think I'm as much to blame as anyone – maybe even more than anyone.

But I trust you. You can decide.

So here's the truth, the whole truth, and nothing but the truth.

* * *

It all probably began before the day Craig Ritchie walked into our classroom, but I don't want to bore you with all the facts about me, and what was wrong in my life. Because that falls into the category of feeling sorry for yourself, and I hate girls who do that. The drama queens. They come into school all red-eyed and you have to ask them once, twice, three times what's wrong, and they won't tell – they enjoy all that attention. Then finally they do and you pass the Kleenex and wait to hear all about how this boy never phoned or some similar crap.

So all you need to know is that my name is Anna Hanson and I was sixteen when it started. Just like most people, I was happy some of the time, pissed off some of the time, but bored most of the time.

I was bored that morning in English. Well, it would have been English if the English teacher was there, but she was absent. On some course. She'd set work. Making notes on the first few scenes of *Macbeth*. Like, who the characters are and the plot and that, who was Thane of what. As if anyone was going to bother. The teacher who was sitting with us brought in piles of marking, and as long as we were quiet, he didn't give a toss what we did. So when I felt my phone vibrate in my blazer pocket, I took it out and read the text under the desk. It was from Karen, who was sitting at the back of the class – there was going to be this big night out on Saturday at the Ritz, I was invited. I replied by saying cheers, I'd think about it.

I didn't want to seem too pleased, too much of a loser. I wasn't one of the girls in the class who was always up for it, but I wasn't a swot either. I was just me, to tell you the truth. I didn't fit into any category. Which was why I wasn't normally included on clubbing nights. So I began to think about whether I wanted to go or not and it was at that point the door opened and one of the deputies came in with this new boy. Everybody stopped what they were doing to have a look. I felt sorry for this lad, being stared at like that. The deputy went on about Craig Ritchie joining this English set and there was a fuss about the regular teacher not being there. The teacher sitting with us was making an empty-handed gesture, as if to say, what do you expect *me* to do, so the deputy grabbed a book off one of the shelves and gave it to the lad.

I watched all of that. The two teachers arguing and stressing each other out, and the boy standing there, head down, shoulders hunched. He was tall and looked more than sixteen. His head was shaved, which surprised me because at our school (St Thomas's – Roman Catholic – very hot on morality and standards and that) boys aren't allowed to have their heads shaved. This boy wasn't in proper uniform either. We wear this awful shade of maroon, but he had a plain black jacket on, over a white shirt. His black trousers were a shade too short for him. He was wearing trainers too, which were also forbidden. In our school they reckon wearing trainers prevents the flow of knowledge to your brain. Only joking. But we do have to wear plain black shoes.

I liked this boy's face. He didn't have eye contact with anyone, but looked alternately at the floor (wooden, varnished over the scratches), the walls (laminated posters of key words – *simile, metaphor, personification*) and the ceiling (polystyrene tiles, a fluorescent light that went on and off intermittently). But his eyes weren't vacant – it was like there was an untapped power behind them. He made me think of a caged lion, or a cornered animal that you had to be wary of, in case he turned on you. I saw him turn his gaze on the class for just a microsecond, and in that microsecond I looked away, scared he might have noticed I was staring at him.

The teacher in charge pointed to the desk at the front by the door and the boy sat there, and then I could only see his back. I couldn't tell, but I don't think he was reading. I think he was just sitting there, turned in on himself, thinking about whatever people think about when they're being private.

It was a bit unusual, I thought, joining a Year Eleven class midyear, and I tried to work out where he could have come from. Had his family moved to Calder?

His arrival had caused a bit of a stir and people had begun to chat. The teacher looked up from his marking and glared at everyone. I glared back at him and enjoyed the flash of uneasiness when he noticed. Immediately I lowered my gaze and made as if I was reading *Macbeth*.

I reckon it's tough being new to a school. School is bad enough anyway – you've got to navigate your way through all the different groups. Paula and Janette are the girls in our year who are in charge, socially, that is. Paula's very streetwise and mouthy; Janette is just a boy magnet. The rest of the girls follow them. Rachel and Elizabeth and some others are swots. Then there's Saira and the other Asians. As for the lads, there's the geeks with computers and GameCubes; the soccer-crazy ones, the skaties and the ones that tough it out at the bottom of the heap, the ones the teachers have it in for.

I was trying to work out where this new boy, Craig Ritchie, might fit in. I would have said in the last group, except most of the boys who just mess around in lessons are idiots, but this lad had a look on his face – he was no idiot. There was more to him. I wondered whether any of the other lads in the class would speak to him at the end of the lesson, but realised they wouldn't. Not yet, anyway.

So when the bell went for break – the teacher with us had been anticipating it and had had his books piled tidily on the desk for the last four minutes – I went over to the Craig Ritchie boy, and said, "Hi."

"Hi," he mumbled.

"You new here?"

"Yeah."

Not the most scintillating conversation, but he was shy and I didn't want to come over like the Spanish Inquisition.

"Where are you from?" I ventured.

"Fairfield."

I knew Fairfield. It was quite a few miles away, a scabby, run-down council estate. No one from our school lived there.

"Why are you here?" I asked.

"Reckon they were forced to have me." There was a hint of a smile on his lips as his eyes met mine. I told him where the drinks machines were, and said I'd show him the way. We walked over to the dining hall, and I filled in the silence by telling him about St Tom's. That, as a school, it was better than most, but it was still a school. And who to watch out for, and what you could get away with. I hoped he'd reciprocate by telling me stuff about him, but he didn't for a while. We sat drinking cans of Coke in the dining hall while people gave us funny looks. They were thinking: *Who's he? Why is Anna Hanson making up to him? Is she that desperate?* People are so nosy.

But to be honest, *I* was nosy about this boy.

"They call you Craig?" I asked.

"No. Ritchie."

He looked awkward in his clothes. The sleeves of his jacket were too short and kept riding up over his threadbare cuffs.

"Are you going to get a uniform?" I suggested.

"No. I won't be here that long."

"Because?"

"School isn't my thing."

"Me neither."

He shot me a quizzical look. I knew what he was thinking. I looked every bit the nice, typical, high-achieving schoolgirl. On the surface, you might even take me for a swot. My uniform is regulation. I don't even hitch my skirt up because that is so sad – everybody does it. I don't wear make-up and have my hair tied back. I do have my nose pierced but I can't wear the stud in school.

"So why are you here?" I asked him.

Ritchie shrugged, then explained. "I stopped going to my old school last year – that was where I used to live. Then we moved. I was pissed off with school, I didn't want to start all over again, but Wendy reckons education's important. She got St Thomas's to agree to have me if I turned up every day and did all the work. So I could take my GCSEs."

"Wendy?" I was puzzled.

"Wendy. My mum."

"You call your mum by her first name?"

Ritchie shrugged again.

"But even then," I said, babbling, "it's really hard to get into St Tom's. There's a waiting list, cos this is a good school."

"Whatever," Ritchie said. "But you haven't met Wendy. She always gets her own way. When she has her mind set on something..."

His voice trailed away. I sensed he didn't want to talk about his mum and I wasn't going to pry. I hated people who did that. So I changed the subject. "Do you know anyone here?"

He shook his head. I reckoned he wouldn't last long. I could see his eyes darting round the dining hall, casing the joint. Like a cat who's out of his territory, trying to get his bearings as quickly as possible. When the bell went for the end of break he said he had to go to the library and do a maths test. I explained where the library was. He loped up the stairs, two at a time, and I watched him go.

CHAPTER TWO

"Are you going out tonight?" my mum asked.

"Yeah, later on," I muttered, my eyes on the TV screen. Until I spoke those words, I hadn't totally made up my mind to accept Karen's invitation. Now I'd committed myself I felt mildly interested in my own decision. I wondered why I'd decided to go.

I suppose one factor was that I just didn't want to stay in on Saturday night. Even though Mum was a bit more cheerful today, the idea of just being glued to the sofa all night and staying up till two or three in the morning all by myself wasn't the most appealing of prospects. Whatever happened in town would be better than that.

But also, I just wanted to give clubbing another shot. I wanted to see if I could enjoy myself more than last time. And to tell you truth, I was grateful to Karen for inviting me. It was friendly of her. A lot of the time I felt as if I didn't have any *real* friends. I get along with people without ever getting close to them. All the girls I know have one other person that they like more than me, a best friend or a boyfriend. Maybe it's my fault and I don't try hard enough, or maybe there's something about me that people don't like – I don't know and, most of the time, I don't care.

Mum was curled up on the sofa, reading some magazine. The sofa is under the wooden staircase that leads up to our two bedrooms. I live alone with my mother in a small terraced house in Calder. You walk in off the street to a tiny porch and then into our living room. It's quite modern with IKEA furniture. You can walk through to the kitchen, and behind that is a small garden. Upstairs there's just our two bedrooms and the bathroom. There's a loft as well, and Mum reckons that one day we could convert it into an extra bedroom and maybe we could have Neil back.

Neil is my brother. He lives with my dad in Exeter. He chose to do that himself when they split up six years ago. He's a year older than me and I get to see him every few months or so. Bit by bit we've stopped being close. My dad remarried and has got two small kids with his new wife. But none of this is a big deal. These are just the facts of my life and I'm luckier than a lot of people. My mum finds it hard to cope sometimes because she gets low – she's off work for stress – but she has her good days too. Today was one of them.

"Let me read you your horoscope, Anna!" she said.

I rolled my eyes. My mum is really into all that stuff big time. As if some freak can work out from the position of the planets exactly what is going to happen to me and the one twelfth of the world's population who happen to be Libra. And they're written so vaguely that you can always fit what is going on in your life to what the horoscope says.

"Here we go," my mum said. *"Today is the first day of the rest of your life. Your voyage of discovery starts here. You're itching for a fight but make sure you don't take on someone bigger and stronger than you. Use your gift for criticism to detect a man who isn't all he seems. And above all, be yourself."*

"Yeah, right," I said.

"Don't be so sceptical. I'm always amazed how uncanny some of these forecasts are. I've been tempted to get my horoscope read properly, taking into account my hour and date of birth. You were born at seven thirty-five p.m. on a Thursday, in case you ever need to know."

My mother's voice was just a little petulant and self-pitying. I know she wants me to be more like her. I can feel her tugging at me a lot of the time to be her best mate, to have girlie heart-to-hearts, to open up and all that rubbish. I would if I thought it would do her any good. Mum already opens up to a lot of people. She belongs to a therapy group and sees the therapist on a regular basis. She does hypnotherapy too, and aromatherapy – basically, if it's got therapy at the end of the word, she'll try it. My mum says that my character is more like Dad's than hers and I can come across a bit shut-off. Which is crap. I'm just waiting for the right person to open up to.

"Where are you going tonight?" she asked.

"The Ritz."

"Who with?"

"Karen, Paula, Janette and some others."

"That's nice."

I forestalled the rest of the questions by giving her a set of answers. "I'll be leaving about nine and I'm getting the bus. We'll share a taxi back around one. I know where my keys are."

"You know not to flag down an unlicensed minicab."

"Yes, Mum."

"And not to have too much to drink."

"Do I drink?" I asked her.

"Well, no, but there's always a first time."

My mum worries too much and seems to think that I'd go off the rails at the first opportunity. The trouble is, she reads too much, too many magazines and newspapers. She believes all these horror stories about teenagers – you know the ones I mean. Teenagers binge-drink alcopops, rot their brain cells with weed while having underage sex and committing copycat crimes from rap lyrics. Sounds like fun. I might try it some time.

But in the meantime, I thought, *I'd better go and get ready for Anna Hanson's big night out.*

A mirror is never enough, is it? You've got to have at least one other person tell you look OK, or better than

OK, if possible. So I went downstairs to my mum and didn't say anything, but stood there, hoping she'd comment.

"You look pretty," she said. "Your hair is nice."

I was wearing it loose. My hair is fair, that nothingy shade somewhere between blonde and brown.

"Why don't you try something with a little more colour, Anna?" Mum suggested.

I was dressed all in black. On Karen's orders. I'd rung her and she said that's how everyone usually dressed. We had to look eighteen and get in past the bouncers. Best not to draw attention to yourself. So I put on a black shirt (three-quarter sleeve), black trousers (plain, New Look) and black trainers. My make-up was lip gloss and a lick of mascara.

"What about that floral-print blouse I bought you from Marks?" Mum suggested.

As if.

I went over to Mum and pecked her goodbye on the cheek and went out. The bus stop wasn't far and I knew a bus was due. Dressed in black as I was, I felt reassuringly anonymous and was glad that no one at the bus stop gave me a second glance, not even the two lads waiting there. I could see the bus approaching, blazing light. I got my purse out of my bag to find my fare.

I like buses at night. You feel like you're enclosed in a separate world, in a little community away from the darkness. I also like the feeling of not being in one place or another, but on the move. Maybe I would have a good time after all, tonight. Anything could happen.

A woman got on with two small kids. I love little kids, the way they stare at you. They came and took the seat in front of me and the little boy knelt on the seat and just looked at me. He was gorgeous, chocolate coloured with large, dark eyes. It's crazy, sometimes I wish I was black so one day I could have a kid like that. I grinned at him and he watched me, a bit suspicious at first. I stuck my tongue out. That made him smile. Then his mum called him and he swivelled round again, and I was on my own.

We arrived at the bus station and everyone queued to get out. I could see Karen and Paula and everyone in a gaggle over by the closed newsstand. I walked over to join them.

"Hi, Anna. We're just waiting for Janette."

Paula and everyone were all transformed. They looked nothing like they did at school. They wore their hair up with huge butterfly clips; their faces sparkled with glitter; Karen had done up her eyes so that they dripped sex. Their perfumes competed with each other, eddies of musky scents moving around them, but overcome by the acrid cigarette smoke – nearly all them were puffing away at cigs. God, I felt dull in comparison.

And just then Janette arrived, stepping out of her mum's Ka.

"You look *gorgeous*!" everyone cried.

Which was true. She did. She just wore a simple black skirt which consisted of a silky lining with see-through flouncy material over it. Janette's top was one of those tight-laced bodices, thrusting up her boobs and leaving a few inches of exposed midriff. I don't blame her – her stomach was flat as a board. She wore black, knee-high boots. All the other girls cooed over her and she chatted away nonstop to them. I had a choice. I could either join in or stand back and lose the sense of kinship that comes from doing the same thing as all of your mates. Because I'm a bit bloody-minded at times – and because I wasn't sure whether I was wanted or not – I stood back.

The Ritz wasn't far. It used to be an old cinema that they converted to a night club. It was the best place to go on a Saturday night. The shaven-headed, puffa-jacket-wearing bouncers gave us all the once-over as we made our way in, but stopped none of us. Karen had warned me they were being more careful since the police raided a few months ago and found the place full of eleven year olds. But it was quite easy to get in if you were female and dressed sophisticatedly. Karen linked arms with me as we entered and that made me feel better.

We paid our fivers at the kiosk and made for the ladies for a bit of extra grooming. I primped my hair a bit in the mirror and wished I'd made more of an effort. I didn't look much different from usual. There were stubs of ciggies in the basins and damp, lipstick-stained tissues. The condom machine had a notice on saying it was empty. Karen said I looked a bit pale and put some of her blusher on me. Then she disappeared into one of the cubicles.

Paula came over to me then and said Karen had fallen out with Mandy and that was why she was hanging round with me. She was only using me. Mandy was there, and was busy fussing around Janette. I reckoned this could be true. Great. I was just a substitute.

We all left together and headed for the bar. They all bought Smirnoff Ices and Vodka Blues. I had a Diet Coke. I don't drink. Partly because I don't much like the taste but, more than that, I don't like what it does to me. I feel as if I'm slipping out of my own control.

The dance floor was quite crowded. The DJ was playing some Madonna track that I forget the title of. Our crowd was still sticking together, shouting in each other's ears stuff about who they knew who'd turned up, what they were wearing, who they were seeing, or every so often their eyes would swivel towards some bloke who'd come in. "*He's* fit! … *He's* cute! … He's *stunning*!"

I just looked around. Karen carried on whispering stuff to me, but I could see that every so often she looked over at Mandy to see what she was up to. I began to feel more and more as if I wasn't really there. It was a strange feeling – as if I was just a pair of eyes, observing. I saw the DJ jerking to the music; groups of lads standing round, bottles in hands; everyone eyeing up everyone else.

I followed the girls on to the dance floor. It was sticky with spilt drink. They put their bags down on the floor so they could watch them while they danced but I didn't fancy that. I kept my bag on my shoulder and decided that I wouldn't dance for a bit, but just look on. Some Ibiza anthem was blaring out now: loud, repetitive music with a heavy bass. The girls were dancing together, showing off their bodies, hoping to attract attention. Paula was getting right down on to the floor. Janette hardly moved. Just stubbing out her ciggie on the floor with the toe of her boot was enough to send the boys wild.

A little voice in my head said, go and join them. Get on the floor and make with the music. But it was no use; I just wasn't in the mood. I was invisible – no one could see me. No boys looked my way. And then I noticed Mandy go up to Karen and say something to her, and Karen hugged her, and Mandy hugged her back, and they started dancing together. I knew what that meant. Bye bye, Anna.

The louder the music got, the more frenetic the dancing, the more detached I felt. Don't think I wasn't having a good time in my own way. I've said before you're not to feel sorry for me as there's nothing to be sorry for. I liked the way my thoughts were coming thick and fast, I liked watching people, I liked watching blokes. If you're interested, I've had crushes on boys and the odd snog, but never a real boyfriend. I want one, one day. You wouldn't credit this, but I have romantic fantasies too. Sometimes I watch old Hollywood musicals on the box, and wish I could be the girl in the long flowing dress tripping lightly down the staircase to the ball, my lover waiting in the hall. Or be the dame in one of those secret agent movies – the woman with a past who the detective falls for – walking into a sordid little office, aloof, sexy, full of passion. Or I'd be on top of the Empire State Building, up high, looking over Manhattan, the man of my dreams by my side and knowing only we two mattered.

How sad am I? I have all the wrong dreams. I know I should want to be Britney Spears or J.Lo, or have a kooky, loving family like in the sitcoms. Or get proposed to on telly or something, so the whole world knows. But when you think about it – when *I* think about it, I mean – today's romance scenarios are crap. All those so-called role models – Britney, Madonna, Kylie – they're just in love with themselves. You can see it on the videos. And everyone is completely into who they pull or have sex with – it's that or soppy look-at-this-lovely-Valentine's-card-he's-sent-me! It's either all crude or makes you want to throw up.

To prove my point to myself I looked again at the dance floor. Some lads had come up to my mates and were groping them. Hands on bums, on waists, and Paula had turned round and was draping herself all over this boy with spiky black hair. They were hoovering each other up with their mouths. His hands were everywhere. It was kind of disgusting and kind of sexy at the same time. I looked away.

Paula wasn't a virgin. She liked chalking up her conquests much as boys do. One lad in our class – Darren – boasted he'd shagged Janette so Paula beat him up. It was the best scandal we'd had in school for ages. But it was all about point scoring, the relationships my friends had. I wished things were different. I thought when I fell in love – pow! – we'd make a new world, a world all of our own.

That crappy world of the Ritz with its bouncers and people gagging for sex they probably didn't even enjoy, the deafening so-called music and the gallons of alcohol, was a pretty rubbishy sort of world. But it was about as good as it got in our town. It was clubbing or looking round the shops at things you couldn't afford. It made me angry. I wanted things to be different, but how could they be? What could I do?

Perhaps I was thinking like that to cover up the fact no one had come up to me for ages. My mates were all pulling lads and I was ignored by everyone. I knew deep down if I'd made more of an effort I could be one of them, but it would mean not being me – it would mean compromise. I don't do compromise.

I wondered if I just went home, would anyone notice? And then the idea of home suddenly became appealing. The club was hot and my shirt was sticking to me. My feet were hot in my trainers. Time was passing slowly. Outside it would be dark and cool and I would be free. Every single one of the girls I'd come with was with someone now, and I noticed a greasy old bloke staring at me. That did it. I pushed my way through the crowd of drinkers and left the club.

It was a relief. I hoped the girls would wonder where I was and maybe even worry about me. If they did worry, it would serve them right. I knew I was supposed to get a taxi home with them, but as I'd left early the buses were still running, so I'd be OK. Technically I wasn't supposed to travel alone at night, but my mum worried needlessly a lot of the time. Most people were OK. It's just the media that want you to believe the streets are full of paedophiles so they can whip up mass hysteria and sell more papers. Everybody's on the make these days.

It was only a short walk to the bus station, down the High Street and then across King's Gardens where the moshers hang out. Another place I wasn't supposed to go at night. It was a square lined with bushes. Each street bordering it had a path that led to the middle, where there was a fountain that hadn't had water in it for years.

Tonight it seemed empty. Maybe it was too early for the moshers – they were probably all at one of their clubs – Medusa's or Hell's Kitchen. I wondered if they also had to pay a fiver for entry. What annoyed me was the fact I'd wasted my money. Five quid entry, two fifty for a Coke, one fifty for the bus. Why was everything so expensive? Where did they expect people like me to get money from? I'm supposed to stay on at school to go to college and not earn money, but also go to clubs, buy the right gear, have a mobile, an MP3 player, a computer. 'Cause people know teenagers want to fit in they target us with all the consumer goods on the market. It just isn't—

I would have said "fair", but I didn't have the opportunity. My conscious thoughts stopped there as in that split second someone ran at me and grabbed at my bag. Pure instinct took over. Not to run – you don't run when someone is trying to take something from you. The instinct is to hold on tight. I did. I also filled with rage – how dare they? They? I looked at my attacker. A bloke. So I kneed him, as I'd been taught to do. Amazing! He let go of my bag and fell to the floor. I'd won.

I was still too full of adrenaline to realise properly what had happened to me. I should have run then, but in an odd kind of way I felt sorry for the bloke I'd just crippled. He was doubled up on the floor. He was wearing trackies, trainers and a hoodie. The hood had fallen over his face so I couldn't see him.

But then he looked up at me.

"Ritchie?" I questioned.

"Anna," he said.

CHAPTER THREE

Knowing it was Ritchie who'd attacked me made me feel better and a whole lot worse at the same time. I could feel myself trembling, and now the initial shock was over, anger replaced it.

"You tried to mug me!" I accused him.

I know this was stating the obvious, but give me a break – someone had just tried to snatch my bag.

"I didn't know it was you," he winced, clearly still in pain.

"So that makes it all right then?"

He didn't reply. Now I began to feel sorry for him. Which was pretty crazy, really – I can be a bit pathetic at times.

"Are you all right?" I asked.

He swore, and told me he wasn't. But slowly he got to his feet. Once he was on a level with me, the situation began to normalise. I was in King's Gardens with Ritchie, late on Saturday night. Ritchie, the new boy in our English set. Never mind that he'd tried to rob me. It almost seemed natural that we should go and sit on a bench together, and he should take a crushed packet of cigarettes from his trackie bottoms pocket and light one, his fingers shaking. He offered me one too.

"I don't smoke," I said.

"I'm trying to give up," Ritchie replied.

The few people who walked past us gave us superficial glances but then ignored us.

"Do you often do this?" I asked him. "Like bag snatching?"

"No. But I need the money. I owe twenty quid to a bloke I know, and if I don't pay tomorrow there'll be trouble. He'll do me over."

I was going to lay into him myself – verbally – for thinking the best way to get money was violent robbery, but something in his manner stopped me. The way he hung his head, the blankness in his eyes – he wasn't mean, but desperate. Plus I was flattered that he'd confided in me. When you have someone's confidence, you don't want to lose it. I didn't feel like criticising or judging him.

"Is there any other way you can get the money? Can someone lend it to you? Your mum?"

Ritchie shook his head. "No. She's hard up at the moment, what with moving and everything."

That was fair enough. Even though my mum was off work, we probably had more money than Ritchie and his mum. My mum would have lent me the money. She wouldn't have been best pleased, but she'd have given it. Ritchie's mum didn't have the money. So if he didn't have a job, and had no one to ask, and he was being threatened with violence, it was hardly surprising he had to resort to mugging. Or was it?

"Couldn't you have just nicked some money without attacking someone?" I asked.

At that point Ritchie looked up at me, surprised. I understood why. I'd surprised myself. Here I was, suggesting he commit another crime – me, who'd never done anything illegal in my life. Except fare-dodging a couple of times, or noticing someone had given me too much change in a shop and not saying anything – oh, and keeping a twenty-pound note I found on a bus last year. But looking at Ritchie's situation from his point of view, theft seemed the only logical answer. But it was wrong. Crime was wrong.

"I tell you what – I could lend you the twenty. It's not a problem."

"But you don't know me," he said. "I might just run off with it."

"Because you've said that, I know you won't."

We both heard the urgent waah-waah of a police car – one followed by another. A typical Saturday night in town.

Ritchie spoke again. "You must think I'm a bleedin' idiot."

"I don't, as a matter of fact."

"Listen, let me tell you. My life stinks right now. First I get all the truant people on my back and my mum stressing about my education, and having to go back to school. I even thought I'd give it a try but it's no bloody good. It's pointless for me – I'm not going to get any GCSEs as I've missed too much. It's all wasted effort. And then the guy I bought the weed from is on my back, and the crazy thing is, the weed wasn't even for me – it was for Loz, my mate. And my other mates – the ones I used to hang out with – before going back to school – I don't see them any more. But they were a load of nutters. Like, what's the point?"

I was stunned. I'd never heard Ritchie utter so many words in all the few days I'd known him. I'd got him down as one of those inarticulate yobs you get (even in our school) but he wasn't, exactly. I mean, how often do you meet a bloke who actually talks to you about his life, and not just the football?

"Look, I'll lend you the twenty quid. I really don't mind. And school's not too bad."

"You're the only person who bothers to talk to me there. Other people just look straight through me. I don't think I'm going to go back. What good is an education going to do me? I'll end up working in some factory or behind a counter – like I said, it all stinks."

"What do you want to be?" I asked him, intrigued. Even though in a lot of ways he was very different from me, I could see we thought in the same way. I felt things were pretty rotten most of the time too.

"What do I want to be? OK, then, how about Prime Minister for a start? Then I'd raze this town to the ground and start all over again, and I'd build houses that people wanted to live in, with gardens and that."

I couldn't help it – I laughed. I didn't expect him to talk like that. But my laughter didn't stop him. He seemed filled with a kind of fury and just carried on.

"Yeah – there'd be no more high-rise flats. You wouldn't have to go to school unless you wanted to, and if you did, you could do what you wanted: paint, or play the guitar, or swim. Yeah, there'd be pools everywhere – free, of course, and free gigs every weekend. And free stuff for kids – shows, and that."

I tried not to show my surprise at his words. I came over all cynical instead. "Yeah, right," I said. "But first you've got to pay off your debts. I'll lend you the money."

"Yeah, but I have to meet this guy tomorrow, and I won't see you till Monday."

"Tell me where you live and I'll meet you tomorrow."

"Why are you doing this for me?" he asked.

I thought to myself, *because I feel sorry for you, because I can relate to you, because by trying to mug me you've pulled me into the drama of your life, whether you wanted to or not. Because even though you sound crazy, I agree with a lot of what you're saying. And because, in a funny sort of way, your life seems more exciting than mine. You take risks, you're brave. And honest.*

I said, "Why am I doing this for you? Because I want to. The end."

"I'll meet you outside the Fairfield community centre at one o'clock tomorrow?"

"Yeah – text me when you're on your way there."

His silence was eloquent. I understood immediately he didn't have a mobile.

"I'll be there at one," I said.

He stood up then and our eyes met. "Thanks, Anna," he said. "And sorry."

"Don't mention it," I said.

I watched him go. He walked quickly, his shoulders slightly stooped, in the way blokes do, the ones who've shot up too quickly. I wondered what he was going home to, and what his life was like outside school. Normally the petty criminals, the kids who get into trouble, go around in gangs. What Ritchie did – mugging me – was well unusual. But then he was unusual too. Saying all that stuff about how he'd change the world. You wouldn't think someone like him would think in that way. Have all those dreams.

You should never judge by appearances.

CHAPTER FOUR

Fairfield looked better than I thought it would, but I guess that was because the sun was shining. It was still a bit chilly – I had my charcoal-grey fleece on. It's sad, in a way, that I don't even have to describe Fairfield to you. Not because it's notorious, but because you've seen so many places like it. Assemble in your mind's eye a few lines of maisonettes with women hanging around outside, two or three grey stone high-rises, and pubs with fat blokes sitting outside on wooden tables, supping beer. But funnily enough, there's a kind of village atmosphere there, because Fairfield is a place a short distance from the centre of town, the nearest we have to a no-go area. So once you're there, it encloses you. You feel part of it. I felt part of it, anyway. I didn't even mind the women eyeing me.

I knew the community centre was a bit further down the road, a one-storey breeze-block building with bars over the windows. As I approached it, I was surprised to see stacks of withered Cellophane-wrapped bouquets of flowers and a couple of damp-looking teddy bears on the pavement outside it. I was trying to read the names on the cards inside the flowers when I heard Ritchie's voice.

"Hi."

I turned. "Hi. What happened here?"

"Some kids crashed a car last month. A couple of them snuffed it."

"Oh." I didn't know what to say.

Ritchie was dressed in an olive-green hooded fleece and jeans. Standing there by all the dead flowers made me feel very alive, spared from something. Almost invulnerable.

"Did you know those kids?" I asked Ritchie.

"No. They weren't from round here."

I put my hand in my jeans pocket then and gave him two ten-pound notes. He took them and muttered some thanks. I tried to make light of it.

"No sweat. I'm always borrowing money off my mum."

"I'll pay you back," he said.

"Whenever."

There was a moment of awkwardness. I thought I ought to go back home but I didn't want to. Ritchie looked different in the sunshine. His shaved head made him look hard, accentuated his jawline and cheekbones. But his eyes – soft, brown eyes – almost seemed to belong to a different person – a shy, uncertain one.

Just at that moment two lads arrived on mountain bikes. One leapt off his bike and stood in front of Ritchie, as if he was barring his way. Ritchie thrust the two tenners at him and he grabbed them. In a second he was back on his bike – it was all over so quickly that if you'd asked me to pick him out from an identity parade, I couldn't have done it.

"I feel shit about taking that money off you," Ritchie murmured.

"Why should you? You were going to rob me of it last night."

"Yeah – but that wasn't personal. Now it is."

For some reason, I liked the way he said the word "personal". I smiled, and still put off saying goodbye. I noticed he wasn't moving either. I wondered if I should suggest we do something. Though God knew what. He didn't have any money and neither did I.

And then the guys on the bikes returned. This time, knowing who they were, I felt my stomach somersault. Wasn't the money enough? Were they going to beat him up after all?

But I was wrong. These were different boys.

"Hiya, Ritch!"

The first one who screeched to a halt and got off his bike didn't look like my idea of a dealer. He wore a local football shirt and had messy blond hair.

"Hi yourself," Ritchie said, looking pleased to see him. The boy with him looked younger – but might just have been shorter. He had a black puffa jacket.

"We're going to Woodsy's place," the football shirt said. "You coming?"

Ritchie hesitated for a moment. Then he said to me, "D'you wanna come?"

You bet.

We walked to a block of flats which looked about ten storeys high. Grey stone, white window frames: not in bad nick, but not the sort of place you'd want to live in. It was dull, uniform, prison-like. I don't know if the lifts were working or not, as the lads made straight for the stairs and ran up them. Have you noticed when lads get together they behave differently from when they're alone? Now that Ritchie was with his mates, he was larking about, competing with them – they were racing up the stairs, calling out good-natured abuse to each other. Luckily I'm quite fit and was able to keep up with them. They – we – ran all the way to the top. I was panting by then. I knew we'd reached the top as in front of us was just a red door and a corridor to our right where the doors to the flats were. But the lads didn't turn right. Instead, the football shirt – Ritchie called him Loz – was messing around with the red door. I didn't see what he was doing, but finally he heaved himself against the door and it gave. It opened to a few more steps, leading to a small room with brick walls and some tanks.

Loz opened another door, and then we walked out on to the middle of the roof.

I watched the lads as they made their way towards the edge. I stayed close to the door; I noticed the place we'd come from was a bricked-in, covered area you could walk all the way round, a self-contained block on top of the roof. Ritchie and the others were at the edge now. I didn't want to follow them. There was no railing, just a sheer drop to the bottom. A CCTV camera peered down to the ground and a couple of aerials stood forlornly.

Then there was the thump of more footsteps and another lad joined us, carrying a stereo. While they were all greeting each other I tried to get over my vertigo. I looked out over Fairfield to the shopping precinct, the covered market and the main road. I turned and could see the park. From up here the whole of Fairfield and its people were insignificant. Being up high gives you a feeling of power. Maybe it was the feeling of power that was making me dizzy. I strained my eyes further to the horizon and saw the hills: tired, worn-out flat hills with the TV mast just a faint line on the horizon. I would have expected it to be windy up on the roof but it wasn't. I could even feel the sun warming my face, making me feel it was all right to be where I was. Bit by bit I left the wall, no longer feeling afraid, but exhilarated. Even, if you like, on top of the world.

"Who's your girlfriend?" one of the lads asked Ritchie.

"She's my mate," he said. "Anna."

Yesss! I was his mate. Ritchie introduced me properly to the lads. The little one was called Tanner. Loz I'd already worked out, and the boy with the stereo was Woodsy. I hoped I was going to remember their names. You know how it is when you meet people for the first time – you're so bothered about what they think of you, you don't focus on who they are. I was wondering what they made of me, and hoped they'd think I was OK. I just wanted to be accepted by them.

I was. The boy called Loz handed me a can of Carling from an Asda carrier bag.

"Cheers," I said, and tugged at the ring pull. I reckoned I could make as if I was drinking it – the last thing I wanted to do was to say in front of these lads that I don't drink. They'd think I was such a square.

We all sat down together, the boys sprawling all over the place, jostling each other sometimes. Loz switched on the ghetto blaster and some R&B played – nothing mainstream, I didn't recognise it. I decided not to talk much. It's better when you join a new crowd just to take note, not to make a complete ass of yourself.

They shared out the Carling and Loz was trying to spray some of the others. They jumped up and ran all over the place. I got a bit nervous when Tanner was close to the edge but I was determined not to show it. Once they settled down, the lads just chatted. Loz was going on about being in town last night and the pub they were thrown out of.

"I thought you didn't have any money?" Ritchie asked.

"I gave my brother a hand in the afternoon with some jobs he was doing," Loz said.

"A hand job, was it?" Woodsy said. Everyone liked that and tried to follow it through with some more comments. I smiled.

"Nah," Loz interrupted. "Stop messing. We did some cars."

"Oh yeah?" Woodsy assumed only casual interest, but you could tell his ears had pricked up.

"Some radios and stuff. I just looked out. Dead easy."

"Nice one," Tanner said, looking impressed.

Loz burped, as loud as he could. The others all groaned. Tanner said, "Watch it, Loz. We got a visitor." He grinned at me. It was a friendly grin.

"Sorry," Loz said. "Where'd you meet Ritch?"

"School."

"That new school you're going to?" Loz asked Ritchie.

He agreed. I noticed he wasn't saying a lot. Was he always quiet like this, or was he just being quiet with me? Even when the conversation moved on to football he didn't join in, but smiled when someone was being funny. Woodsy was going on about someone they knew who'd got in a fight with what sounded like a neighbouring gang. I couldn't quite follow.

But what I noticed was that they'd accepted me. I mean, whoever was talking sort of included me with his eyes. With some of the gory stuff about the fight – this guy lost four teeth – they specially looked at me to see my reaction. No one was playing any games. I thought of Karen and how she used me, and of all the girls at school and their allegiances and bitchiness. In contrast, these lads were dead straight. They weren't clocking me to see what I was wearing, they weren't ignoring me, nor were they putting me in the spotlight. I know you'll have them down as a band of yobs, petty criminals and all that, and I'm not denying that they were, but they also had good manners. They put me at my ease. And it was great up there on the roof, in the sun, away from everything small and petty. I didn't even need the Carling to feel drunk.

Tanner was explaining how to get to someone's house when we could hear more footsteps. This time the lads looked bothered. They began to curse and we all leapt up, realising we'd been discovered. And there was only one way down.

"Where are you, you buggers?" came a gruff, angry voice.

"Come and get us," Ritchie taunted.

Then he pulled me round the building to the door,

guessing rightly that our pursuer would chase us in the direction of his voice. The other boys followed. We ran round the building, shot back inside and headed for the stairs. As fast as we could, almost tumbling, we catapulted ourselves down the foul-smelling concrete stairwell, round and round, down and down, until we hit the lobby.

"Let's split," Ritchie said.

Everyone ran off in different directions. Ritchie took my hand and walked slowly away with me. I could see what he was doing – making out as if we had nothing to do with trespassing on the roof, just a boy and a girl taking a stroll. Appearances were everything.

It didn't matter, as no one came to run after us. We walked towards the precinct, not that the shops were open. I was feeling great – adrenaline was coursing through me and it created a big surge of happiness. At the back of my mind a rather tinny voice prattled, *You shouldn't have gone on the roof. It was trespassing and it was dangerous.* But I didn't care. I thought – what harm did we do anyone else? Why shouldn't we go on the roof?

Once we reached the precinct Ritchie dropped my hand, and commented that we were safe now. He laughed, and I could tell he was in the same mood as me. If anything, the weather was sunnier. I just wanted the day to go on and on. When Ritchie suggested the park just outside Fairfield I tried not to sound too eager.

We walked up to the main road, crossed at the lights and made our way to the park entrance.

"So they're your mates?" I asked him.

"Yeah, they're all right. Tanner's all right."

"Did they go to your old school?"

"No."

We reached the park gates. An ice-cream van was outside with a straggling queue. I was remembering what Loz had said about breaking into cars. The slight jolt it had given me had gone. It left me curious to know more.

"So where did you meet them?"

"Around. We hang out together during the day – *used* to hang out together when I first moved here, before I went back to school."

"They wagged it?"

"No. They just didn't go to school."

We were walking along the main path that led to the centre of the park. Ritchie turned off to the left on to a narrower path that led to the lake. The ground was slightly uneven and I had to watch my footing. Once we came to the lake, it was easier. We headed for a bench and sat there. Further down a man and a boy were fishing, a dark green tent beside them.

"But I thought everyone has to go to school by law?" I questioned.

"Yeah, but not everyone does." Ritchie lit a cigarette, and with each drag he became more talkative.

"I hated my last school. Everyone had it in for me. The teachers, right, you can tell they have favourites and I wasn't one of them – no way. It was quite interesting, some of the stuff we did, but then half the time some old teacher would rush through the explanation when you were copying from the board or when the class was talking, and then refuse to repeat it, so I didn't understand what was going on. Then they tell you off more and call you stupid. And you get to believe it after a while."

I told him that was dreadful and St Tom's wasn't like that, but I knew I was lying. A few of the teachers treated us as if we were pretty hopeless, thinking that would encourage us.

"So I used to wag it," Ritchie continued, "and then everyone would be on at me, so I'd go back to school, but by then I'd missed so much I couldn't be arsed to catch up. And even the other kids treat you funny, like you don't really belong. So you find you're acting even more of a prat in order to get accepted."

Ritchie laughed to himself.

I prompted him. "Go on."

"Like this. There was this one teacher, Conner, taught science, who kept picking on me all the time. He really pissed me off. He asked me questions when he knew I didn't know the answers, he made jokes about the stuff I was wearing and if anyone was talking, he'd be, like, 'Ritchie! Get out!' I hated his guts. So what I did, I got myself locked in the lab one lunch time and loosened the tap on the front bench. So when we had our lesson after lunch, he starts this experiment and goes, '…and you have to add some water', turns on the tap and it shoots off right up in the air, and he gets soaked with water. Completely drenched. All over his face and shirt. It was just brilliant. The class was in hysterics."

"Did he know it was you?"

"I didn't wait to find out. I legged it and didn't go back. I reckon they didn't think it was me as there was nothing on my records when I started at St Thomas's. It was all about having to come in every day. Making a commitment, all that crap."

"I'm still surprised our school agreed to have you."

"You wouldn't be if you'd met Wendy – my mum. She was the one who arranged it. All that stuff about you've got to give him a second chance, and he needs a good school, and look how high his SATs marks were."

"It's good your mum cares about your education," I commented.

"Yeah. She cares, all right."

"Do you get on with her?"

Ritchie looked baffled for a moment, as if no one had ever asked him that question before. "Yeah, yeah. I do. She can be hard to live with, but she's my mum."

I could relate to that. I was quiet for a bit and stared ahead at the lake. Then I thought it was sad that Ritchie hadn't had a proper education up till now, and then I thought that a so-called proper education wasn't all it was cracked up to be. Half of what I was learning for my GCSEs was going to be useless to me. And so much of the time I switch off in lessons – we all do. It unsettled me, the way Ritchie was making me see things differently. I had to admit he might be right about schools. But surely it couldn't be right to steal, and that's what he and his mates did. You see, at that point I still felt things like stealing and vandalism were wrong.

Ritchie carried on talking, telling me about his mates. None of them went to school either. Tanner had been relentlessly bullied and the school couldn't stop it. Loz had been excluded lots of times. Woodsy used to go to a special place for kids thrown out of school, but he even refused to go there.

I asked him what they did all day. Ritchie lit another cigarette.

"Hang out in town. And we watch what's going on, where they're careless about security. We've nicked a few things. We know some people to pass them on to."

I could tell he was trying to impress me. There was a slight swagger in his speech. After having admitted he'd opted out of school I suppose he felt the need to show me he was smart. But I told him he'd get into trouble,

...dn't defend theft. He turned then and ...straight in the eye.

...ken. In my life what have I taken? A few packs of ..., stuff that's been left around where any fool can see it, cash if I can find it. And what's been taken from me? Everything. I've got no future – I know that. I live in a stinking hole of a flat with my mum, who was kicked out of her job because the pub landlord wanted a younger barmaid – he robbed her of her income.

"Everywhere you look, people are on the game. Businessmen, politicians, builders – everyone's on the make, everyone's only out for number one. Even the bloody *Big Issue* sellers pretend they haven't got change if you offer them a fiver. So tell me why I should be any different?"

At that moment a toddler set up a wail near us and I heard his mother screaming at him. But his wail drowned her voice. I tried to think what I could say to argue against Ritchie and came up with nothing. Looking at life from his point of view, I could see why he'd made his choices. They now seemed perfectly reasonable to me.

"My mum's out of work too," I offered. "Through stress. She's normally a practice manager for some doctors, but she gets periods of depression, ever since my dad left. He lives in Exeter with my brother. I don't get to see them very often. Do you see your dad?"

There was a beat, and Ritchie said, "I saw him the other day."

"Yeah?" I encouraged him.

But Ritchie's face had darkened into an ugly scowl. I backed off. I could see I'd accidentally soured the atmosphere, and that was the last thing I wanted to do.

"Let's drop all this shit," Ritchie interrupted. "I'm not a loser – even though you think I am."

"I don't," I said.

But the atmosphere had changed, unmistakably. We both left the bench and walked on along the side of the lake for a while, saying nothing. A few clouds had appeared, though it was still a nice day. I tried to lighten up by telling him about school and trying to make him laugh. And I succeeded, and he told me about the books he'd been reading and about the punk tapes he collects, music from the seventies. He liked The Clash and The Adverts. He said just because he hadn't gone to school didn't mean he was braindead. He read the papers when he could. The more we were talking, the more I was beginning to see that Ritchie was my superior – he'd lived more and even read more. He'd had tough choices and he'd thought about things. I felt shallow in comparison. But that wasn't a bad feeling. It made me determined to be more like him – that wasn't a conscious determination. It was just his influence working on me.

We sauntered all the way to the gates at the other end of the park, which happened to be near my side of town. I knew I ought to offer to go, and I did. I asked Ritchie if he'd be in school tomorrow. He shook his head and I felt a rush of disappointment.

"Why?"

"It isn't right for me. Maybe when I'm older, but not now. I've got to get my head straight first. But, Anna, I owe you some money."

I was glad. It was a bond between us.

"Meet me at the shops near school at four. By Music Zone."

I told him I would, and meant it. He turned and went back through the park. I began to walk in the direction of my house but I found I didn't want to go home. I would have like to have stayed with Ritchie. This had been the best afternoon I'd had for ages. I wanted his life, not mine. Only we were so different – but were we?

I had a lot of thinking to do.

CHAPTER FIVE

When I got home, I could tell my mum was feeling bad again. Sundays often got her like that – Sundays are pretty depressing for anyone, but my mum beats herself up about being off work and how it's all her fault. She was sitting in the kitchen when I found her, cradling a cup of tea, her voice nervous and weepy. She asked me whether I'd managed to get any shoes and for a moment I hadn't a clue what she was on about, until I remembered that was what I was supposed to have borrowed the money for.

"No," I said. "I'm going to carry on looking."

"I should have gone with you," she said. "I'm such a bad mother."

I told her she wasn't. She disagreed, and said the proof was that she was off work on sick pay. I tried to argue with her but it was no use. In this mood, she keeps knocking herself all the time. Like a dog tied to a pole, she goes round and round in circles, treading the same ground. Dad left her because she wasn't good enough for him, she ought to work on her self-esteem but what is there to like about her, life was just a black pit and she was at the bottom, what could she do to get out?

This might sound dreadful to you and maybe you're feeling sorry for both us, imagining I get upset when my mum gets upset. I did in the beginning, but now I find I cut myself off and I don't feel anything. It scares me sometimes, that I don't feel anything. I just wait for her to stop. I do try to tell her positive things but I know from experience she won't listen. Sometimes I feel resentful and I want to scream: "I'm only sixteen – what do you expect me to do?" Or I start thinking traitorous thoughts, like, you could help yourself if you want to. For example, Mum won't take anti-depressants because she says they're drugs and she's scared of being dependent on them. Instead she does all this therapy stuff.

But she was crying now so I knew I had to do something. I gave her a hug and said she ought to ring Julia and have a chat. That shows how desperate I was. I can't stand Julia. Mum met her at the therapy group. She's got more money than sense and too much time on her hands, as her husband is rolling in it. She doesn't go to work, and her hobby is working on herself. She not only goes to the group therapy sessions, but she's in private analysis with the therapist, and is in training to become a therapist herself. It's a nice little business. A lot of money changes hands.

I realised I was starting to think like Ritchie. But he was right – he was so right. Here was my mother, ill and in need of help, and – hey presto! – here were lots of people eager to help her: her therapist, her hypnotherapist, her masseuse, all charging piles of money, feeding off my mother's problems. Julia didn't charge Mum anything, though. She just encouraged my mother, which is in some ways worse. But that night I wanted time alone, and I thought that Mum might as well ring Julia and let her listen.

I brought Mum the phone, went upstairs, and decided to run a bath. I love soaking in the warm water, preferably with a layer of bubbles. What I do is stare hard at the bubbles and the rainbow colours in them, and imagine each little bubble is a world in itself, with millions and millions of inhabitants no bigger than atoms. I've done that since I was a kid. Then I smash the bubbles like a vengeful god.

I lay back in the water, replaying all the things that had happened in the last twenty-four hours. But I'm not really one for thinking about the past much; I'm more interested in the future. I was glad I'd be seeing Ritchie again. Then asked myself, why? Do you fancy him? I moved some of the bubbles over my exposed body.

I liked him, definitely. I felt we were very similar in some ways. The fact he operated outside the law was frightening and exciting at the same time. I also suspected he had opened up to me in a way that he didn't with his mates. Opened up. Yeuch! A phrase of my mother's. I mean, we talked a lot, and it was good. And, yes, I liked his face, and I had to admit, he wouldn't have had this effect on me if he was a girl. Which might mean something. But now all I wanted was his friendship, and I wasn't going to risk that by introducing all that stupid boyfriend/girlfriend stuff. Like he said, we were mates. And that was more than good enough. Anyway, it felt all wrong, me and Ritchie dewy-eyed, in *luuurve*. That wasn't what it was all about.

The water was cooling now so I heaved myself out of the bath, took the largest towel and wrapped myself in it. School would be bearable tomorrow because I had something to look forward to at the end of it. I debated whether to get straight into my pyjamas even though it was only five, and spend the rest of the night chilling. But that seemed a bit of a slobby thing to do, so I went back to my room and got back into my jeans and a sweater.

It was lucky I did, because when I got downstairs, Julia was there.

"Anna darling! Come here. Let me kiss you. No – both cheeks. You look gorgeous. Anna – your poor mother. What shall we do with her? I thought rather than speak on the phone I'd come straight round and be here for her."

I forced a smile.

Julia was sitting on the sofa with Mum, holding both

her hands. It made me feel a bit sick – jealous, even – and so I let a sarcastic comment out.

"How's your non-specific anxiety disorder, Julia?" This is what she claims to be suffering from. In plain English, that's worrying needlessly.

"Thank you for asking, honey. I'm making progress. I understand now that it comes from caring too much – it's the result of a caring overload."

Oh, puh-lease!

"Anna," my mum said. "Can you make Julia a drink?"

Grudgingly I asked the traditional questions. Tea? Coffee? Milk? Sugar?

"Do you have anything herbal?" Julia asked. "Camomile would be a joy."

I was waiting for the kettle to boil when my ears picked up the tune of Celine Dion's *My Heart Will Go On*. I was puzzled for a moment or two, until I realised it was Julia's mobile ringtone. I made a retching motion to myself. Then I heard her chatting to Geoff, her husband, confirming my suspicions. Julia's voice was loud and brash, and it carried. When she finished the call, she carried on making my mum feel better.

"It's not at all surprising you feel the way you do. It takes a long time to recover from a failed marriage. Years and years and years – sometimes a lifetime. And the pressure you were under at work – I never understood how you managed to cope at the best of times. But

Monica – I've been thinking – do you think you might have an underlying medical condition, like ME? Your immune system is probably depleted. Mine is, you know. I've been seeing a wonderful nutritionist who's advised me on the best vitamin combinations and food supplements. You ought to try her. Hang on."

I could hear another mobile ringing. What was this? This one played some pan pipes New Agey tune.

"Kathie? Darling! Yes, of course I can make bridge on Wednesday. But, honey, I can't talk now. I'm on a mercy mission. Ciao."

Bitch, I thought. I walked towards Mum and Julia with a tray of tea and biscuits. And yes, just as I thought. Julia had not one but *two* mobile phones. I caught her explanation to Mum.

"One is a private line for me and Geoff. The other is my public phone." She took her tea from the tray and turned her wide eyes on Mum. "Now, Monica, tell me all about it. You know I'm always here for you. Don't hold back, honey. Let it all come out."

I couldn't stand another moment. I could feel myself getting into a pretty bad mood. It was impossible to stick around. I went back upstairs, stomped into my room and set about making it Julia-proof. I put on some music and got out my geography coursework. I always liked to be on top of things at school. There was less trouble if you were, and I didn't mind the work. The kind of stuff we had to do at GCSE came pretty easily to me, but I wasn't a swot. I did what I had to do. Which is kind of my motto, I suppose.

I did what I had to do.

Even through my Green Day tape I could hear Julia's voice, because she was standing at the bottom of the stairs.

"Now remember what I said about positive thinking and Bach flower remedies. And ring me any time of the day or night, honey. Do you know, I think I've done you the world of good. You look so much brighter since I came in. Keep it up!"

Then I heard my mum's voice, and she did sound brighter. I was both pleased and annoyed about that.

"Anna! Julia is going now."

I knew that was a coded request for me to come down. There was no escape. I didn't have a choice – I had to go down and be nice to Julia whatever I might be thinking about her and the way she used my mum. So I made my way slowly down the stairs and saw Julia with her jacket on, her bag over her arm, standing by our front door. She kissed us both effusively and we watched her walk down the front path to her silver baby Volvo. My mum had always taught me it was polite to wave visitors off. Julia got in the driver's seat but then my mum shouted to her.

"Julia! I forgot to give you the book I mentioned, *Believe and You're Halfway to the Stars*."

"Don't come out!" Julia called. "I'll come back and get it. Anna – keep an eye on the car!"

Julia ran past me back into the house, and being allergic to her presence, I strolled out to her car, noticing she'd left the keys in the ignition and the door slightly open. *Silly woman*, I thought. You should always lock a car if you're leaving it, even just to post a letter. A thief could be in and out in a second.

Which made me think of Ritchie and I smiled.

There was Julia's bag on the passenger seat. A Louis Vuitton, would you believe? Her bag was even unclasped, and you could see her two phones on the top. *Two* phones. And Ritchie didn't even have one. Seeing both of them lying there made me think how easy it would be to take one of them – say, the Nokia with its silver cover. I could see my hand as if in a diagram, reaching into the car, lifting the phone, and inserting it into my jeans pocket. Not that I'd ever *do* anything like that – it was just that I could see how it *could* be done.

I wondered if I had the guts to do it.

Quick as a flash there was the cool weight of the phone in the palm of my hand, and then its neat pressure on the side of my thigh. I still stood by the car, but now my breathing was shallow and my heart was pounding. My knees were weak with fear. I heard Julia's voice again.

"Thank you for this, honey. You're right – I'm sure it will help me. I do need to work on my affirmations. I must dash now – as I said, dinner party this evening!"

We passed each other on the garden path. She gave me a conspiratorial grin. Something made me stand there and watch her get into the car. If she noticed one of her phones was gone, then that would be it. The game would be up. But she didn't bother to look at her bag at all, just drove straight off.

The fear that had been semi-paralysing me now dispersed like ice melting. I felt an exhilaration like I'd never experienced before and also, though this will sound crazy to you, a sense of justice accomplished, as if I was right to have done what I had done. That Julia deserved to have her phone nicked, and that I had taken something that belonged rightfully to me. I have to admit there was an insistent pressure in my mind, a voice asking me, *What will happen when she finds out the phone is missing?*

"I feel much better now," my mum said. "Thanks for suggesting I ring Julia. I tell you what, I'll go and make something for us to eat – how about an omelette?"

"Yeah," I mumbled. "That'll be nice." Then I thought, if I act at all odd, my mum might suspect something. That was when I discovered the first rule about being a successful criminal. Act innocent. Don't give a thing away.

"Yeah – I'd love an omelette. Have we got any ham and cheese to put in it, otherwise it'll be a bit plain? I know there are some oven chips left."

"That's a good idea," my mum said, grinning at me. "I'll put the oven on right now."

"I need the loo," I said.

I did. It was true. My stomach was tied in knots. But I didn't feel guilty. There wasn't space. I was so wild with fear and excitement, I couldn't tell which was which.

All I knew was that my life had just become a lot less boring.

CHAPTER SIX

You don't want to hear about my day at school, about the girls fussing around me and asking what happened on Saturday night. I made light of it and didn't bother to comment that one of them should have rung me yesterday if they were that worried. You also don't want to hear about my Monday timetable, how I overheard one of the deputies mentioning to the Head of Year that she'd noticed Craig Ritchie hadn't turned up and ought they to check. You might want to know that the Nokia was in the internal zipped-up compartment of my school bag, and that I kept my bag close to me all day.

After school I went to the shopping precinct near school and stood by Music Zone.

They call that precinct The Broadway – I suppose to make it sound like something cool, some place you would find in the US of A. But really it was just like every other shopping precinct in the country. It had: New Look, Top Shop, Marks and Spencer, Greggs Bakers, Woolworths, Martins Newsagents, Dorothy Perkins, Etam and so on and so on. In the centre was a square, with one side giving on to a covered market, which was open three or four days a week. In the centre of the square was a statue of an old bloke pointing towards Music Zone. There was a low wall around the statue with quite a few people sitting on it. There was one dreadful moment when I thought Ritchie might not be one of them, but thankfully that moment was short-lived, because there he was. The waiting was over and my life was beginning again.

He smiled when he saw me and moved along so I could sit by him. The stone was cold and my feet didn't quite touch the ground. It was weird: even though I'd been thinking of little else but Ritchie and stuff all day, now I was with him my tongue was tied. I couldn't decide what to say to kick the afternoon off.

So it was Ritchie who spoke first. "I've got something for you," he said, reaching in his jacket pocket. He brought out a handful of money, a couple of fivers, some pound coins – I didn't see how much and didn't bother to count it. It embarrassed me, receiving money from him.

"I'm only taking this from you," I said, "because I borrowed it off my mum. Anyway, where did you get it from?"

Ritchie's lips curled into a smile and I knew there was a story attached.

"Last night I went to this pub I know – I don't have trouble getting in because I can look eighteen all right. I waited till closing time and there was this bloke pissed out of his head. So I told the bloke behind the bar I'd help the drunk off the premises. He was stinking with booze. He asked me to get him a cab and I did."

"So he paid you for that?"

"No. I went through his pockets."

For a moment I was shocked. A beat later, I felt an illicit thrill. Anyway, I was just as bad, and was about to prove it.

"I've got something for *you*," I told Ritchie. I delved into my bag, got out the phone and presented it to him. He looked puzzled at first and asked me if it was mine.

"No," I said. "I nicked it."

I loved the look on Ritchie's face then – incredulity, admiration, appreciation. He held the phone in his hand and considered it while I gave a brief account of what happened with Julia.

"She rang my mum when she got home," I ended, "to ask if she'd left her other phone at our house. Me and Mum had a good look for it. Julia said it must either be in the car or else – because she'd left her bag open – it must have dropped out and she hadn't noticed. Either way, she told my mum, it was only a material possession. It was replaceable and she wasn't going to let its loss activate her non-specific anxiety disorder. She'd just ask Geoff to buy her a new one."

"Cool!" Ritchie said.

"We just need to check if it's unlocked and if it is, we can get a new SIM card for you."

"SIM cards cost about fifteen quid," he commented.

This was true and I was silent. I knew Ritchie had just given me twenty pounds, but it was my mum's money. She still expected me to buy shoes with it, and I told Ritchie that.

We sat quietly for a while, watching the shoppers walk by us. Then Ritchie commented, out of the blue, "I never expected you to do this. I don't want you to get into trouble."

"Oh, I won't," I said teasingly. "I'm a good girl – no one will suspect a thing. I've never been in trouble in my life."

"Yeah, but stay that way, Anna. You don't want to end up like me if you can help it."

I wanted to say, "I do!" But that would have sounded so childish. And I didn't like the way Ritchie was drawing a line in the sand, so to speak, between me and him. I'd come over to his side now, and I wanted to explain that to him.

"No, listen. I was thinking about a lot of the stuff you said yesterday, and I reckon, you're right. This isn't a fair world we're living in. Loads of people with money don't deserve it, and people who do deserve it, don't have any. Taking Julia's phone was only like redistributing wealth. Like taxing. And you – nicking money off that drunk bloke – well, he shouldn't be drinking so much in the first place. You've taught him a lesson. If he was sober, he would have kept his cash. Maybe when he woke up this morning and realised what happened, he decided never to drink again. And you changed his life for the better. I know it sounds crazy, but it might be true!"

I could tell Ritchie was accepting what I was saying. I was pleased. But the truth was, I was kind of making it up as I went along. I was desperate to keep Ritchie, to align myself with him and no one else. Then I began to think that maybe what I was saying was true after all. Stealing wasn't always a crime, depending on who you stole from and what you did with the things you stole. It stood to reason. And coming up with this justification felt good. I could see it made Ritchie feel good too. I was excited now, and carried on.

"It's like Robin Hood – taking from the rich to give to the poor. And he was a hero, wasn't he?"

"But *you're* not poor," Ritchie said.

"Yes, but I can still be on the side of the poor," I argued. "And because I don't look like a thief, I'm more likely to get away with it, you see. I think I'd make a brilliant Robin Hood." I was half messing, half serious.

"No," he said. "I'm Robin Hood. You're Maid Marian."

"Whatever," I said. "But I don't see why I can't be Robin Hood too." It was like we were kids, squabbling over who was going to be who in a make-believe game. Because that was exactly what it felt like to me at that point – a make-believe game teetering on the edge of reality.

"Because I've had more experience than you, Maid Marian."

That riled me. It sounded kind of sexist, if you can see what I mean. I knew I had to prove myself. I had an idea.

"I know how we can get the money for your SIM card."

"How?" Ritchie challenged.

"The money you gave me – it was for shoes. So I need to go home with a pair of shoes – then we can keep the money. I'm going to go into Shoe World opposite and nick a pair. Then we'll get the SIM card for the phone."

"You're joking."

Good! I'd succeeded in surprising him. "I'm not joking. It'll be a cinch."

I could feel the same terror and excitement coursing through me as I did when I nicked Julia's phone. It was hard to breathe. I tried to steady my breathing and clear my head so I could think how I was going to do it. Then Ritchie spoke. "It'll be easier if we do it together. And plan it out beforehand."

"But Ritchie, if you come in with me, people will suspect us at once. I don't want to be mean or anything, but…"

The fact was, he looked like a criminal. With his hoodie and trackie bottoms and shaved head, the security guards would be on him as soon as he walked in the shop.

"That's my point. I'll be the decoy. While everyone's watching me, you can do the business," he said.

He was right. And I liked the fact there was some moral justice in that. If all Ritchie had to do was walk into a shop and people were going to suspect him just because of the way he looked, then they deserved to be hoodwinked. The nice girl examining the black trainers would really be the thief, and they wouldn't even notice. Serve them right. And Shoe World could stand the money. They were a chain that had outlets in all the shopping centres round here. And their shoes were pretty rubbishy anyway. Poor shoes for poor people.

We sat watching Shoe World for a while, casing the joint, and making some plans. Ritchie said it was important to be observant and not to rush it. Timing was everything. He said there were some shops that were walkovers, others that were harder to tackle. He didn't know about Shoe World, but it was worth taking the risk.

The longer we sat there, the more sick I felt. But talking through our plans helped. Once you visualise it all happening, all you have to do is walk through it. Ritchie said that most people are pretty stupid when it comes to preventing theft. People who worked in shops were most often not the owners but poorly paid part-time sales assistants, and it was no skin off their noses if the stock was depleted. I told him about a lesson we'd had at school last year about where trainers were made – nearly all of them, both branded trainers and cheap ones, came from the Third World, and the kids who put them together were paid the barest minimum, and worked fourteen hours a day sometimes.

Ritchie said, "We'd better get on with it. If we leave it much later, the shop will be empty."

First I tidied myself up. I put my school blazer back on, took my hair out of its ponytail, brushed it, and tied it neatly back. I checked my prefect's badge was straight. I looked every bit the product of St Thomas's R.C. school, a pillar of the community. Meanwhile Ritchie threw his hood over his head.

I left the statue first. I spent a little time looking in the window of Shoe World, then I entered. Shoe World was one of those discount-type shoe stores. It consisted of rows and rows of shoes sorted into men's, women's and children's, then into smart and casual, and then size order. It was like a library of shoes. There were about nine or ten people milling around, looking at the shoes. There was one girl at the till and two male assistants keeping an eye on things, though they couldn't see everywhere because the racks of shoes were so high. There was that rubbery smell you associate with shoe shops.

I made my way over to the trainers and began to scrutinise them. I decided it would be best to pick a pair around the twenty quid mark so my mum wouldn't suspect anything. In a normal shoe shop, you only get one shoe of the pair out on display to deter thieves. But that requires more staff to go and hunt out the other shoe, so shops like Shoe World took the risk of having both shoes in the pair on display so they could cut staff costs.

Now when I smell shoes, I always think of that Monday afternoon in Shoe World. I selected a pair of slip-on black trainers with a small loop on the back. I held the shoes in my hand and looked at them. Then slowly and deliberately I made my way to a stool where I could sit down to try them on. I checked that my school bag was unzipped. It was. I left my old shoes by my school bag, walked over to a mirror propped on the floor against the wall, and examined the look of the new shoes on my feet. Actually the trainers weren't all that bad. They were neutral, nothingy. They would do for my new life.

I knew as soon as Ritchie walked into the store. The sales assistant nearest me had been staring aimlessly, but now focused his gaze on the new arrival. I looked up briefly to check it was Ritchie, then carried on inspecting the trainers I was wearing. I even smiled at a woman nearby me, to establish my right to be there.

Luckily she moved off shortly afterwards. That was a risky thing to have done. I saw the sales assistant moving closer to Ritchie and making eye contact with his colleague, as if suggesting he should also be keeping an eye on the villain who'd just walked into the shop. Ritchie walked over to the men's trainers, keeping his face well hidden in his hood. I wouldn't have trusted him either, looking like that. The two sales assistants closed in on him.

Then, all of a sudden, Ritchie shouted, "What are you staring at me for?"

Everyone in the shop turned to look at him.

"What am I doing wrong, eh? Ever since I come in here, you've been giving me the eye. You got it in for me, haven't you?" And there was more. His voice got louder. He swore a bit. One of the sales assistants tried to get him out of the shop.

Then, in a deliberate movement, I put my old shoes in my school bag and strolled out of the shop in the new ones. I even stopped outside the shop to watch the disturbance with Ritchie, saw one of the sales assistants arm-lock him and pull him towards the door while the other one attempted rather pathetically to frisk him. What did they think he could have stolen in that time? Were they complete airheads, or what?

I walked off in the direction of McDonalds and stood outside. Time was suspended for me. I couldn't say we'd been successful until Ritchie escaped. Each second dragged interminably. My mind was blank. Then Ritchie arrived beside me.

"Like your shoes," he said.

In reply, I kicked him in the shin.

CHAPTER SEVEN

I know you disapprove. You think that nicking those shoes was wrong, and the truth is I have to agree with you. Which is why I'm telling you all this. But at that time, the wrongness of what I did was what made it work for me. I felt as if I'd outsmarted everyone by not playing according to their stupid rules. Also, because it was wrong, it bound me to Ritchie. It was our secret. Nobody else knew what we were up to – at least, then. And besides, the very next day I had the glimmering of an idea how I could salve my conscience.

But first I have to tell you what happened when I got into school on Wednesday.

Paula came up to me with that look in her eyes, the one girls get when they're getting ready for a good gossip. "I saw you down The Broadway yesterday afternoon," she said.

I went scarlet. I thought, *She knows. She saw us in Shoe World. The whole thing's over*. Seen through Paula's eyes, our escapade with the shoes seemed shoddy, cheap, worthless and common.

"Go on, then," Paula continued. "Spit it out. What were you doing with that new boy?"

So she didn't know. It was Ritchie and me together

she saw, and she thought I was going out with him. By this time a little audience had assembled, consisting of Janette, Karen and Mandy. Mandy was chewing; every so often you could see a flash of white as she moved the gum around in her mouth. Janette was applying lip balm with her index finger.

"What's going on?" squealed Karen.

"That Craig Ritchie is Anna's new bloke," Paula stated.

I was surrounded. I could feel their combined curiosity tugging at my secret. But I played it cool. "He's not my bloke exactly," I said. "He's a kind of mate."

"You're a quick worker," Paula said. "So why's he not been in school? You got him hidden away somewhere? In a little love nest?" It was hard to tell with Paula whether she was being straight or sarky.

"Yeah," I parried. "Doing my every bidding."

All the girls laughed. I was glad. I'd said the right thing. Even though I'm a girl myself, girls in a group make me nervous.

"Why hasn't he been in school, Anna?" Karen continued.

"He got fed up," I said.

"Can't blame him," Paula commented, losing interest.

"But are you going out with him?" Karen nudged.

I just smiled – enigmatically, I hoped. Because at that precise moment in time I wanted to think I was going out with Ritchie. It was probably pure vanity and a desire to impress the girls, mixed up together. But then, if I hadn't fancied him, the sheer thought of us being an item would have disgusted me. Ritchie didn't disgust me. The opposite, in fact. There was something hard and definite about him that made him more real to me than anyone else in my life.

Then the teacher came in to take the register and the usual chaos ensued. I was left with a sort of glow. I was happy. The happiness persisted throughout registration, all along the corridor and up the stairs to the English room, and even during the lesson itself. It was still *Macbeth*. The bottom sets only saw the video and looked at a scene or two. We had to read the whole bloody thing. And discuss it with the teacher. The swots were getting into their stride.

"But what I don't understand," Rachel said to Mrs Keane, "was why Macbeth never told Lady Macbeth he was going to get Banquo murdered. Because she would have approved. She was harder than him."

Rachel loved doing that – spotting stuff in the text that nobody else did. Mrs Keane enthused accordingly.

"Absolutely! Another of those little puzzles that Shakespeare loves to leave us."

"She wasn't just hard," Elizabeth added. "I would say she was evil."

"Now where's your evidence for that?" Mrs Keane asked. The three of them usually kept any discussion going all lesson. Elizabeth supplied the evidence, but I was feeling mutinous. I didn't much like the swots and, anyway, I thought they were wrong about Lady M.

"She isn't evil," I said. "She loved Macbeth, and she wanted what he wanted even more than he did."

"Interesting!" gushed Mrs Keane.

But I wasn't going to say any more. I understood only too well what was going on in Lady Macbeth's mind. I recognised that denial – the way you pretend to yourself and the way you pretend to others. I guessed she also had that feeling of walking a tightrope, and not looking down for fear of losing your footing. Yeah, I could relate to Lady M – which was weird. I wasn't evil, was I? Lady Macbeth was, because she said that gruesome stuff about killing her own babies if she had to. And also, she was ambitious. And selfish. No – I wasn't like her. Me and Ritchie were different. Like we'd said, we weren't the Macbeths. We were Robin Hoods. From now on, I vowed, we'd pick and choose our activities very, very carefully. And we wouldn't benefit from them. We'd make sure others benefited. We'd operate outside the law, but for the right reasons. So I decided to text Ritchie at break now he'd got his phone working and ask him to meet me later. There were things I wanted to talk about and plans I wanted to make.

*   *   *

"Helping people?" Ritchie's voice was incredulous.

"Why not?" I countered.

It was raining and so, of all places, we'd ended up in the Launderette in Fairfield. There was a small parade of shops – chippie on the corner, newsagent's, hairdresser's, a boarded-up shop and the Launderette. The smell of washing powder pinched my nostrils. The machines clanged and clattered as we talked. Sheets and towels and pillowcases and T-shirts getting cleaner and cleaner by the second.

"Like you've said, it's unfair," I explained. "Life's unfair. But we're good at what we do – the way we got those shoes yesterday. We could make things a bit more fair. Ritchie?"

His face was unreadable and it made me uneasy. It reminded me how little I knew him. Funny how you can be obsessed with someone and think about them pretty much all the time, have the most important experiences of your life with them, and not know them. I'd picked up that Ritchie was a fairly private person. He'd told me hardly anything about his home life apart from those few, sparse facts in the park on Sunday afternoon. He lived alone with his mum; it sounded like he had a bit of contact with his dad, though they probably didn't get on well. Maybe he was waiting to know me better before he told me more. This was reasonable. I had to be patient. Which was fine, really it was fine. Had he spilt everything out to me at the beginning, I would have valued him less. His reserve made him attractive to me.

"You do fancy him!" teased an inner voice.

"Well?" I persisted. I dug Ritchie in the side with my elbow.

"Explain what you mean exactly," he said.

"Well, like, if we knew someone, someone who'd had a hard time, or who needed money. And we made things better for them, or found them some money. By maybe nicking something and giving it to them."

Ritchie looked thoughtful. "Taking it from someone who deserved to be ripped off. Some bastard."

"Yeah!"

He laughed, and I felt I was getting somewhere. One of the washing machines banged repeatedly and then came to a halt. The silence seemed to expose us, and I found myself whispering.

"Do you know anyone who needs a few quid, Ritch?"

"Me. I need a few quid."

"Apart from you."

"Lemme think."

Two women came in then and gave us a suspicious once-over. So we got up. The rain had stopped anyway. We walked until we came to the main road and sat on a wall by the bus stop.

"What I can't stand," Ritchie said, "are the bastards who nick stuff off old people. You know, the ones who pretend to be gasmen or plumbers and get inside their houses and take their benefit books. It's like taking from your own. A few weeks ago this old lady near us let these blokes in who said they were council workers. They nicked loads off her. We know about it because she stops and tells everyone. We should get the bastards who conned her."

"That might not be possible, but couldn't we get back some of her money?"

This was more like it. Ritchie and I were thinking as one again. That was what I liked best. The traffic swished past us on the wet roads. I know I was prattling a bit, but I was excited.

"We could go back and do another shop – not in Fairfield, somewhere else, in case we're recognised. Just me and you. Maybe in town. But the problem is, we need money, and it's not easy to steal money, is it? What can we do?"

"To get money," Ritchie said, "you need money. That's how big business works. It's how *we* could work. You know, I heard of this idea, once, only it's pretty complicated."

"Spill," I instructed him.

This couple walked into the bookshop – you know the one – there's a chain of them, there's probably one where you live. But I'm not naming names, for obvious reasons. But this couple – they were obviously students. The bloke was wearing a black and white bandanna, tatty black sweater and jeans. The girl with him – his girlfriend? – had a rucksack slung over one shoulder, a copy of the *Big Issue* poking out of the top. She wore some black Bench trousers and a Kangol T-shirt. Her hair was in cutesy little bunches. The couple didn't stop and look at the special offers and recommendations at the front of the shop, but made for the stairs and went to the first floor, where the non-fiction was.

"It's a matter of seizing your opportunity," Ritchie muttered to me, rubbing his bandanna where his scalp was itchy.

"Uh-huh," I said to him. "I've checked out the ceiling. There aren't any CCTVs."

"Bookshops are cool because, if you're lucky, you can rip out the security strips, if they're stuck to Cellophane," he commented.

Also, I thought, bookshops were cool because they were mainly arranged in alcoves. I cast my eyes over to the cash desk where there were two assistants. One was dealing with a customer but the other was staring idly into space. We made sure we had our backs to him, looking as if we were just browsing.

"How do you feel, Anna?" Ritchie asked.

"OK. Good." Which was true. I was completely happy. I loved being with Ritchie like this. I was totally focused on what we were about to do, living completely in the moment. I checked my rucksack was open, and took a moment to calm my breathing. Ritchie steered me over to the alcove in the far corner. A notice read, *Psychology*.

"Find a book that there are several copies of," he said. "Something we can afford."

We'd scraped together all of our available resources: the money mum gave me for school, including twelve quid for a theatre trip I was supposed to be going on, some change lying around the house, and some money Ritchie said he was owed by Loz's brother, which I didn't ask any questions about. We had just over thirty quid with us in total. I began to browse through the psychology shelves, Ritchie standing guard protectively. I knew he was giving the cash desk sidelong glances.

"*Educational Psychology Today*, that's twenty quid. *Psychology and Social Policy*, thirty. *Crime and the Individual*, fifteen. *Young Offenders*, twenty. *Understanding Crime in Modern Society*, thirty. There are five copies—"

"Now!" urged Ritchie.

I'd been waiting for this. In an instant I tore off the security tag and shoved the book in my rucksack. Time stood still. My heart was beating like a hammer and icy fingers squeezed my stomach. If we were going to be spotted, it would happen now, at this precise second. But all was quiet. All I could hear was Ritchie's heavy breathing and a distant conversation. I couldn't help but turn to look at the cash desk. One of the assistants had his back to us, involved in some transaction. The other was off in the opposite part of the shop, helping a customer. Ritchie had chosen the moment well.

As we'd planned, we began to make our way out of the shop. Not too fast, but not dawdling either. My knees were trembling and to steady myself I linked arms with Ritchie. I felt his reassuring squeeze. That was good.

Outside the dusk was falling. I was full of adrenaline and wanted to run, or hit out, or hug Ritchie. But I did none of those things. I concentrated on seeming as normal as possible and we continued to walk to McDonald's, and entered.

Tanner was already there, sitting at a table drinking a huge chocolate milkshake.

"Gimme a slurp," said Ritchie, and helped himself.

Rather him than me. Chocolate milkshake was the last thing I wanted. My excitement made me feel slightly sick. We passed the rucksack over to Tanner, who peered inside.

"You're weird, you guys," he said.

"Just wait," Ritchie commented.

In the beginning I hadn't wanted Tanner in on what we were going to do, but Ritchie explained the advantage, and then said, if we were going to make a habit of this, we'd need support. We'd need a gang, he said. And then it felt OK. Me and Ritchie, and our gang. Our homies, our brothers. He said Tanner was the most trustworthy. Because Tanner had been bullied, he made the most loyal friend you could have. He really appreciated people who were nice to him. I gave him a friendly smile, and reminded him that we'd see him in Burger King in half an hour. He nodded, and said he hadn't forgotten.

Afterwards Ritchie and I walked up and down Church Street. Church Street was the main shopping area in town. It was chain-store heaven. Marks and Spencer, BHS, Debenhams, Starbucks, Wetherspoons, you name it, it was there. I linked arms with him again. It occurred to me I might be being a little too friendly, but I didn't mean anything by it – it was more that I just *had* to link arms with him. I felt close to him. That was all there was to it.

I wondered what we'd be doing when this evening was over. I thought I'd like to meet his mum, and see his house, but I could hardly invite myself. Still, if the opportunity did arise…

I found I couldn't keep quiet any longer. Nervousness loosened my tongue. I just had to talk.

"So Loz, Tanner and Woodsy – are they your only mates?"

"More or less. There are some others. But I'm not the type who needs friends much."

"I'm the same. Have you ever had a girlfriend?" I blurted out.

"Not a proper one," he replied. I was pleased about that.

"The bandanna suits you," I said.

"You don't look too bad yourself."

I tried not to show my pleasure. Anyway, it was time to adjust our appearances. I took my hair out of its bunches and let it hang loose, while Ritchie removed the bandanna. Soon we found ourselves outside the bookshop again. Time for Round Two.

We entered. This time we did stop to look at the displays of bestsellers. Ritchie said he'd read a book once called *On The Road*, which was pretty cool. I'd not heard of it. He also said I should read *Brave New World* and *1984*. I was interested that Ritchie liked reading, only I didn't ask him more because I had to keep my mind on the job. I just asked him what he thought of *To Kill a Mockingbird*, which we were doing at school. He said he'd read it a year or two ago, and that it was good. I noticed most of the books on sale were silly girlie romances and crime novels. We carried on chatting as we made our way to the psychology section. This time when we looked over to the cash desk we smiled at the assistant. In fact, I broke away from Ritchie and went straight up to him. The assistant was very thin, pigeon-chested and spotty.

"Where's the psychology section?" I asked.

He pointed to it and seemed very friendly.

"Oh, thanks," I gushed. "I've got to get some books for college. I'm starting a new module. Cheers!"

I walked over to psychology, trailing Ritchie. We found the same bookshelf we were at before, but this time had a fairly audible conversation.

"My module's on crime, and I've got this long essay to write."

"Have you got your reading list with you?" Ritchie asked.

"Oh, shit!" I put my hand over my mouth as if I hadn't wanted that word to slip out. "I've left it in the flat."

"Do you remember any of the titles on it?"

"Well, kind of. Most of them had 'crime'."

Ritchie made an exasperated gesture and glanced over at the assistant, who was watching us. Ritchie rolled his eyes, as if to say, women!

I began to pick out books and leaf through them. I took *Understanding Crime in Modern Society*. "This one looks good," I said. "It's a bit hard to understand in places. But I'm fairly sure this one was on the list."

"What are you gonna do?" asked Ritchie.

"Ooh – I don't know!" I went on, doing my best ditsy impersonation. "I really don't know."

"Look, why don't you get it anyway," Ritchie said, as we made our way to the cash desk. When he spoke again, it was half to the sales assistant. "If it turns out to be the wrong one, you can always bring it back. She can get a refund, can't she?"

"Certainly," said the bloke at the till.

I got out my purse, and we all chatted as I completed my transaction. This bloke had just started there full-time, after having backpacked in Australia. I told him Ritchie and I were at the Central Uni, I was doing psychology and Ritchie was into Business and Management. The assistant popped the receipt into the bag, we thanked him profusely, and left.

Now Ritch and I were on a high. We got out of the shop and hugged each other – our first hug. I was exploding with happiness. Ritchie seemed full of energy, humming to himself, a spring in his step. There was Burger King, and inside we saw Tanner, with yet another choccy milkshake. That boy was going to be seriously ill. We opened the bag from the bookshop and gave him the receipt.

"You know what you have to do," Ritchie said to him.

Tanner gave a smart salute and it made Ritchie smile.

"Jump to it, then!" The lads were messing and it was good to see. Tanner sucked at the straw in the milkshake, making a revolting sound as the last of the shake vanished into his mouth. I pulled a face. Tanner shot off on his bike.

"Fancy a coffee?" Ritchie asked me.

"Not here," I replied.

We went next door to Coffee Republic. We had enough money left for one coffee between us. Ritchie queued up for it while I found a table at the back, in a corner. When he brought the coffee over, he came and sat by me. We were side by side, our legs touching. We took sips from the coffee in turn.

"All these gaps – this waiting around – makes me nervous," I confessed.

"It doesn't bother me," he said.

"You're good at this. The acting, I mean. Anyone would think you really were a student."

"I will be, one day."

That was interesting. I prompted him to continue. "I might study acting," he said. "At some college or other. I reckon you don't need qualifications for that, just talent. Once I get out of here, that's what I think I'll do. When it's all over."

"When what's all over?"

"Stuff," he said, drumming his fingers on the table. Then he changed the subject. "Are you rich, Anna?" he asked.

"God, no. But we're not poor either, sort of in the middle. That's why – up till now – I'd never thought of stealing—"

"Shhh!" warned Ritchie.

"Of doing what we're doing."

"Taxing. Taking our cut."

"Taxing, then. But, tell you what. You can see for yourself how rich I am. Come round to mine some time."

"I might," he said. "You know, your hair looks nice like that, just loose. It makes you look older. Come on – it's time."

"OK," I said, tingling with excitement.

So we got up and strolled back to the bookshop. We marched in, through the shop, up the stairs, straight to the cash desk. And our luck was in, as I knew it would be. Because Ritchie and I together, we were charmed. The Fates were on our side. Nothing could touch us. The same assistant was there, and when he saw us, he grinned in recognition. Poor bastard. He actually seemed pleased to see us. We were probably the nicest customers he'd had all day.

"You're not going to believe this," I said to him.

"It was the wrong book?"

"Too right."

Ritchie stood there looking bored, as if being linked to an airhead like me was getting him down.

"What is the right title, then?" the assistant asked. "Can I help you find it?"

"*Crime and Society*," I said. "But I hope you don't mind – I've decided to get it out of the library. I'm ever so sorry. The truth is, when I checked my bank balance…" and I ended with a giggle.

"Can you give her her money back?" asked Ritchie, as if he was beginning to lose patience.

You could see the assistant clocking the situation. Ritchie was getting more annoyed by the minute, and there was this feeling that we might start rowing if I didn't get my money back.

"Have you got the receipt?" the assistant asked.

"Sure," I said, fishing around in the bag with the book inside. "Hold on a moment." I fished some more. "Heck, I can't find it."

"Here – let me," Ritchie said. He took the book out of the bag, examined the bag, examined the book. "What have you done with it?"

"Sorry! It's not my fault. Please don't get angry."

"You should have been more careful to keep the receipt if you weren't sure about the book! And you've thrown away the wrapping!"

Ritchie sounded seriously annoyed now. I could see the assistant getting more and more edgy. "Look," he said. "It's OK. I remember you buying the book. I'll give you a refund and explain to my manager. He'll understand."

I shot him a happy smile. "See?" I said to Ritchie.

"Thanks, mate," Ritchie said to the assistant.

He opened the till, completed some paperwork and handed us one twenty and one ten-pound note. We thanked him, and left.

But it wasn't over yet. We walked quickly away from the bookshop to the end of Church Street. There was Tanner on his bike. When he saw us he felt in his pocket, and handed Ritchie a twenty-pound note and two fivers.

"It was a cinch," he said. "Even though the other branch didn't have a psychology section, they said that since I had the receipt, they didn't mind refunding me the money. You ain't half clever, you two."

Ritchie handed Tanner back a fiver. That was his commission. Which we could afford, as we'd doubled our money. Once we'd replaced our own cash we were left with twenty-five quid clear profit. How clever were we? But the best was yet to come.

On our way to the bus station we saw a *Big Issue* seller. As usual, everyone was ignoring him, keeping their distance, as if he was scum. As if they were so much better than him. We went right up to him.

"Here you go, mate," said Ritchie, handing him a fiver. "It's OK, we don't want a mag."

"I've got one," I added, waving mine.

You should have seen the look on the bloke's face – like it was five Christmases all rolled into one. I'd never seen anyone look happier.

"Cheers! Good luck to you!"

We grinned and hurried off. We broke into a run when we saw the bus to Fairfield ready to depart. On the bus we relived our scam, replaying every second, everything we said and did. In no time, we were at our destination. We jumped off the bus and Ritchie took me by the hand.

"This way!"

A row of rather shabby maisonettes, plastic dustbins outside them. One house towards the end, with a light still on in the kitchen. The doorbell wasn't working. Ritchie rapped on the glass panel in the front door.

We heard footsteps and a chain being inserted. The door opened just an inch or two. A suspicious old-lady voice said, "Who's that?"

"It's Craig Ritchie, Wendy's lad."

"What d'you want?"

Her voice sounded less suspicious. She recognised him. "I'm not letting you in, you know. They came last week, the men from the council. They took my benefits book and my jewellery and my purse. You can't trust anyone any more. I'd be better off dead, I would."

"I've come to give you this," Ritchie said. "We've been having a whip-round – me and my mates." He handed her the twenty-pound note.

At first there was no response from her. I said, "Go on – it's for you. Not everyone's bad. Please accept it. You can treat yourself to something."

She unchained the door and opened it. While she gave us a good stare I took in her cluttered hallway and inhaled the fusty old-woman smell of her house.

"Take it," Ritchie said.

A small, wrinkled hand reached out. "This is good of you," she said.

"Don't mention it," I said, preparing to go.

"You're good kids," she said. "You're good kids. There should be more like you. I'll tell them, I will. I'll tell them when they start complaining about the kids these days, all into crime. I'll say, I know two decent kids. God bless you!"

"You too," I said, as we walked away.

CHAPTER EIGHT

If you could have seen the look on that old woman's face, you wouldn't be sitting there thinking I'd done wrong. That bookshop wouldn't have even *noticed* the book had gone missing. Thirty quid to them is a spit in the ocean – twenty quid to that old lady was a fortune. And it restored her faith in human nature. She said so.

You can imagine the mood I was in that evening. The only thing that dented it was that Ritch had to go – he'd said he'd arranged to do something with his mum. He didn't say what, and it's only now, when I'm remembering it all, that I realise he didn't look me in the eye when he said that. But then I probably thought he was embarrassed – I mean, it's a bit soft for a lad, having to go somewhere with his mum. So I thought nothing of it. We went our separate ways that night, which was just as well. It was good that the evening ended just there. Anything else might have been an anticlimax. We just smiled at each other – I mean, really smiled – and I ran as fast as I could to the bus stop.

When I got home Mum noticed the change in me. "You look happy," she said, a shade enviously.

"Yeah, I am."

"Any reason?"

I'd got into the habit of acting now and so this one was easy.

"Yeah. I've been getting on better with the girls at school. Paula asked me over to her house and we all watched a video and had pizzas. It was Karen's birthday. We had a good laugh. I think I'll be seeing a bit more of them now."

Mum grinned. "I'm so glad to hear that! I always thought you should mix a little more and I've blamed myself – that you were ashamed of me and didn't want your friends to meet me."

"Mum!"

She laughed ruefully. "Why don't you invite them over here?"

"I might," I replied. "But also there's this lad I've met."

"Anna!"

I smiled and dropped my eyes. My mum carried on prodding me for information. I just said he was one of Paula's gang and there wasn't anything in it – yet. That he was quite good-looking and he went to our school for a bit. That I just wanted to take it slowly for now.

"Quite," said my mum. "Never throw yourself at a man. Well, who would have believed it? Your first boyfriend! Do you know, you're making me feel a whole lot better!"

Which just goes to show, doesn't it? What me and Ritch were up to was even making my mum better! So I said I'd get on with my homework and I went to my room. I looked over some of my science for a test we were having but I couldn't concentrate. All the stuff we'd said and done was whizzing through my mind. So I left my work for later when I couldn't sleep and went to the bathroom. I realised I still hadn't opened the present my brother Neil had sent last Christmas – a set of soaps and lotions and that. It showed how little he knew me – thinking I was into all that girlie stuff. But now, I felt like using them. I carefully removed the Cellophane from the soap – it was called *Bathing Beauty*. I sniffed it. Kind of lemony and ginger. Not bad. I turned on the hot water tap and, when the temperature was just right, I held the soap under it, and then rubbed it in my hands. It lathered nicely. I put the soap on the side of the basin and washed my hands, enjoying the sensation of the thin film of soap between my fingers, making the skin soft and clean. I stayed there for quite a while.

I didn't see Ritchie for a few days. I was careful not to text him too much because I didn't want to spoil the balance of our relationship. And also I wanted to give it a little break so I could get on with the rest of my life. It seemed important to me to build a kind of alibi, to go to school, work hard, not to let anyone know that I'd changed. That I had a secret. Well, secrets, really.

So I learnt stuff for tests, finished my coursework, all the time acting the perfect student and daughter. I could afford to. Because whenever something went a little too wrong – one of the girls ignored me at lunch and chose someone else to sit with, or if my mum had a low patch, or if the bus was late – I would think, if only you knew. If only you knew who I really was and what I really did. So I was waiting, waiting for the next time me and Ritch went taxing.

I wouldn't have imagined that the next episode would start because of my mum, but it did. She wanted to go to visit her friends at the practice she managed, or used to manage. She'd been feeling a bit better lately and was even talking of going back to work. She asked me if I'd come with her because she was scared she might have a panic attack. I agreed – why not? My reward, I decided, would be to allow myself to text Ritchie later. Just the thought of that buoyed my mood and meant I was prepared to put up with anything.

So there we were in the waiting room of her surgery – well, not *her* surgery, but you know what I mean. Although the practice was about to close for the evening it had been a busy day and there were still a few patients waiting to see the doctors. Mum looked a bit nervous, and I knew she felt odd being in front of the reception desk when she should have been behind it. I gave her hand a friendly squeeze, and she squeezed it back.

Luckily there was a distraction at that moment. A woman came in with three kids, one in a buggy and two more holding on to the sides. She recognised Mum and a conversation started. It was funny how being thrust back into her professional role brought my mum out of herself. This woman and my mum had a private, urgent conversation from which I was excluded. So I watched her kids, which was fine by me. I like kids.

The baby in the buggy looked like she was teething. Her cheeks were red and she was chewing on a trainer mug. Her eyes were dull and she didn't react to my grins. She only looked mildly interested when I stuck out my tongue at her. I reckoned she was probably the ill one. Her older brother and sister had gone straight over to the toys. In the waiting room there's this big red box full of battered toys, plastic garages, dented spinning tops, big wooden jigsaws with half the pieces missing. But these kids didn't seem to mind. They were in there, seeing what they could find. The boy brought out a sad-looking teddy bear with a bandage round its ear. He stared at it, then threw it to one side. He picked up a plastic tractor and examined it. Then found an old Action Man. He sat himself down on the floor with it and was soon involved in some imaginary game. It was cool watching him. Meanwhile his sister had bonded with a scrappy old doll whose plastic eyelids kept falling over her baby blue eyes. She was talking to it and holding it. It was brilliant watching those kids play, to see how they lost themselves in those toys. When the receptionist called the woman for her appointment the children refused to be separated from their finds, and I could see a nasty situation beginning to take shape.

"If you want to leave them here I'll keep an eye on them," I offered.

Mum explained who I was and the woman looked at me with gratitude, then wheeled the baby off to the doctors' rooms. Mum popped into the office to see her old friends, and I was quite content, watching the kids. The little girl started singing something to the doll, then sat her on the floor and began putting all the other toys around her. The boy had picked up a book and was looking at the pictures. I would have gone over to help them play but it was clear they didn't need me.

Time passed quickly. Mum and this woman came out pretty much at the same time. When the kids were separated from the toys they'd chosen they predictably set up a wail. The mum looked seriously harassed. She ended up smacking both of them. That made them wail even louder.

I asked Mum, "Who are they?"

She explained on our way home. The woman lived in one of those B&Bs for the homeless. But that was an improvement on where she'd been before, which was a refuge for battered wives. Now they were living in one room until she could get fixed up with a council flat. She was offered one but it was too high up, on the twelfth floor of a tower block and she turned it down, because of the kids. What would she do if the lift broke down? That seemed fair enough to me. The kids were so young she couldn't go out to work and they lived on benefits.

When she was explaining this to me Mum began to sound like her old self. I was pleased about that, but also saddened and sickened by what she told me. You'd think the government or the council or somebody would help that woman. Because her situation wasn't her fault, and it certainly wasn't the kids' fault. But she seemed to be getting the barest minimum. And it was a treat for her kids to go to the doctor's surgery, for heaven's sake! That tatty old toy box was a treasure chest for them.

And then I had our next idea – well, it was my idea, but I couldn't have carried it out without Ritchie, as you'll see.

I texted him and we met at the parade of shops near my part of town. I was there before him and waited anxiously. When you really like someone you're always scared they won't turn up when they say they will. But Ritch was only five minutes late. He wore a navy tracksuit I hadn't seen him in before. I wondered for a moment if it was new and he'd put it on for me. Because the truth was, I'd taken a little bit more care than usual with my appearance. My hair was down and I wore my new black denims.

"What's up?" he said, grinning, looking pleased to see me.

I grinned back at him. I wanted to keep this cool, and get that same buzz we always had when we were plotting things.

"I had this idea," I said.

He took out one of his ciggies. I kind of took a mental snapshot of him at that moment – that's how I always see Ritchie. Lighting up a ciggie, dressed in his navy tracksuit with a white stripe down the side, lounging in the doorway of the shuttered chemist's, the flame of the match flickering and suddenly illuminating his features.

"Like, last time we helped that old lady. Why don't we do something for kids this time?"

"Kids?" He frowned at me.

"Yeah. Poor kids. Kids whose parents can't afford to buy them toys. Listen – this is what we could do. I could print out an official-looking letter on my computer asking for donations of toys, and we could go into all the toy shops with it. If we dress up right and act dead grateful they'll never guess."

Ritchie stood there thinking for a while, then began to smile. "You're mad, you. What's the point of that? That's just charity – that's not what we're up to. We tax, remember?"

I was instantly deflated because of course he was right. I'd wanted to go out on the streets with him so much I hadn't been thinking straight. There was no thrill in just being charity collectors. But I felt honour bound to defend myself. I didn't like coming off worse in an argument.

"Yeah, but *we'd* be the ones who decided where the toys are going to."

Ritchie shook his head. I was getting desperate. I started ranting at him. "We'd still have the power. And then people might give us money too, instead. Because, when you come to think of it, all the charities you read about, they don't give all their money to the people they say they're helping – they keep some of it for themselves – their wages, and that. Overheads, that kind of stuff. And the people who give to charity are big hypocrites – they give to Oxfam then go round the supermarket overloading their trolleys. Or give to the NSPCC and hit their own kids. And that reminds me – the woman I saw – the mum. She was having such a hard time. And it wasn't her fault – she'd come from a battered wive's refuge. And her baby was ill – you could tell just looking at it."

Something I'd said had caught Ritchie's attention. He wasn't laughing at me any more. "So what's your idea again?" he asked.

It might have been simple, my idea, but, boy, was it effective!

We started in Robinson's, the toy shop in my part of town. You should have seen me. I put on my suede skirt, brown, just below the knee, with a dusky pink sweater. Ritchie had on a pair of plain black trousers and a navy sweater. We debated about his baseball cap and he argued that if he didn't wear it we'd be in danger of looking like two Jehovah's Witnesses and it would alienate people. So I said he could go with it.

This was the letter I'd written and printed off. I made up a sort of headed notepaper as if it came from a youth group – I called it St Margaret's, as I thought it would be good to have a saint in it. I made up an address in Redvale, another part of town. Then it went like this.

Dear Shopkeeper,

The St Margaret's Youth Action Team are collecting for our Toy Appeal. We are asking you for donations of toys, which will be given to local children's hospitals and hospices to brighten the lives of our young people who are suffering.

Here is a plea from Emily, who is five, and has kidney failure:

"I hate being ill, but playing with toys makes me feel a lot better. But all the toys in our ward are old and the nurses can't buy any more."

Make a child like Emily's face light up with your donation…

I was pretty pleased with that. All those English lessons on how to write letters and how to argue, persuade and advise had paid off. I'd signed it as the youth group leader and it all looked pretty official. But I reckoned – rightly, as it turned out – that people are too embarrassed to check all your credentials if you say it's for charity. I'd even printed out little cards for me and Ritch with false identities – his read Ross Angus, and mine, Jaime Somers. Because I liked that name.

So we walked into Robinson's and I explained to the woman behind the counter about the appeal. I said I wasn't expecting them to give us new toys, but maybe damaged stock or something. I was quite loud so two or three of the customers in the shop started listening, and they all had those goofy expressions on their faces, as if to say, "Aaah! Isn't that sweet?"

So naturally the woman behind the counter, who turned out to be the manager, had to give us something. While she went into the back room, the people in the shop asked if we would accept money as donations and Ritch said that would be no problem.

The manageress came back with a couple of dolls and some plastic gladiator figures with an arena for fighting in, as well as a collection of jigsaws. Ritchie put them all in the sports bag he was carrying. I gushed a bit to make it all authentic.

"It's so kind of you," I said. "Could you sign this form with a list of what you've given and the shop's address, please. You've been so generous, I can hardly believe it! This is so much more than I expected." The more fuss I made, the more attention I attracted. The more attention I attracted, the more people who came over, had a look at what we were up to, and forked out.

Ritch and I were over the moon when we came out.

"It's so bloody easy!" he said.

"Let's try Play and Learn."

It was the same story there. I did get a bit nervous when the girl in charge rang head office to authorise the store's gifts, but there didn't seem to be a problem. She even apologised that they were only giving us discontinued items. We amassed shape sorters, a slightly torn playmat and pretend kitchen equipment. Ritchie had now got into the swing of it and actually made an announcement to all the customers about our collection. They were falling over themselves to give something. One mum gave her little girl a fiver and told her to give it to us for all the poorly children. This little girl waddled over to me and shyly proffered the note. I thanked her very much.

At Bromley and Bromley's, the posh toy shop – that had designer clothes for kids, would you believe! As if a toddler would know he was wearing Nike or Timberland! – as the assistants were giving us stuff, the manager began to ask us questions.

"I've not heard of St Margaret's Youth Action Team, and I live in Redvale."

My stomach flipped. Luckily Ritchie answered.

"Because we've only been going a few weeks. My dad started the group. He's a local vicar."

I thought that was risking it – maybe this manager was a churchgoer. But he seemed reasonably satisfied. Then he asked another question.

"Which hospitals are you giving the toys to?"

That was OK. I knew my hospitals because of Mum and rattled off a list. Then I tried to stop the questioning by blabbing on a bit. "We're going to go round the hospitals after school tomorrow. One of our leaders is going to take us in her van. Everyone's been so generous."

"I don't remember reading about this in the papers," the manager persisted.

I could feel myself getting hot; beads of sweat were forming on my temples. Yet the strange thing was, the more scared I got, the more inventive I became.

"The papers! You're so right! We should have let them know what we were doing and then we could have got extra publicity. And asked the readers for donations."

"Tell you what," the manager said. "I can ring the *Echo* now and get a photographer round. Then they can run the story next week and appeal for toys from the readers."

It was then I was more scared than I ever had been. I'd never believed my mum when she said she was having a panic attack, but now I knew exactly what one felt like. How on earth could we explain that the last thing we wanted was publicity?

"Jaime!" Ritchie said condescendingly. "You're such an airhead. Sorry about this." That last comment was to the manager. "There is a story going in next week. A reporter came round, but you forgot, Jaime."

Ritchie had thrown me a lifeline. I grabbed it eagerly. "Because I wasn't there! I had a dental appointment, you idiot!"

"Thanks, mister," Ritchie said. "We have to go now. Sheila said she'd meet us in the van."

And as quickly as we could, we got out. I thought I was going to throw up, but the feeling gradually subsided. As my terror diminished, it was replaced by the realisation we'd got away with it – again. My ruse had worked – we'd ended up with more toys than Father bloody Christmas. It was amazing – completely amazing.

Correction: I was amazing, Ritchie was amazing. Nothing could stop us now. I was overwhelmed with euphoria, like I'd taken a drug. I offered to take one handle of the overstuffed sports bag that Ritchie was holding.

"Where shall we go with these now?" I asked him.

"That's all been taken care of," he said.

"Don't be mysterious." Because we did have a bit of a problem here. My house was out of the frame as my mum would start asking questions. I presumed the same would apply to Ritchie's place. We needed to stash the toys somewhere before we distributed them.

"I had a word with Loz," Ritchie said. "He gave me the key to his brother's old office."

"What office?"

"A minicab office. They rented it for a while but they couldn't make it pay. But he had one of the keys copied. It's empty – you'll see."

CHAPTER NINE

We came out on to the main road, the one that leads out of town. It was getting dark now but the stream of traffic was still fairly constant. You know the road I mean. It just exists for cars – most of the shops are permanently closed and the ones that still trade have their graffiti-splattered shutters down at night. I remember seeing a garage – lights blazing – in the distance, a late-night grocer's shop and a takeaway advertising kebabs, curries, pizzas and fish and chips.

Ritchie scanned the street. We finally came to a halt by a pale-blue door by the side of a boarded-up shop front. He put the bag down, got a key out of his pocket and opened the door to darkness. He fumbled for the light switch, there was a tiny blue flash from a loose connection, and then I saw in front of me a dirty corridor with a single, bare electric bulb hanging from the ceiling. A door to the right obviously led to the office, but Ritchie took the bag and ran up the stairs facing us. I followed him.

At the top of the stairs was a toilet – the door was open. It looked pretty vile. There was a room on either side, and more, narrower stairs leading to the top storey. Ritchie opened the door on the right and we went in.

The room looked as if no one had been in there for ages, the sort of room that had forgotten what people were like. A white, Venetian blind covered the large window that looked out over the main road. You could hear the rush of traffic from where we were. I saw a wooden table with a couple of mugs on it, permanently stained with coffee rings, two kitchen-table-type chairs and an old easy chair with one of those grotty floral loose covers. There were some wooden packing crates. The floor was linoleum, pitted with little holes where people had stubbed out cigarettes. It smelt damp and musty, but I could also detect the stink of old alcohol and the unmistakable aroma of weed. Ritch closed the door and we were alone.

We were alone. That fact transformed this grotty room. What you might think was sordid, seemed exciting to me, full of possibilities. Ritch and I were in our own, private place. And it wasn't too bad, not really. I reckoned that, given a mop and a bucket of soapy water, I could make something of it. I walked over to the blind and peeked between the slats down at the main road. It was like spying. No one knew we were there.

"Let's have a look at what we've got," Ritch said.

I turned and saw him swing the sports bag on to the table. We took out some of the toys and talked about what we'd done, reminiscing. I confessed how scared I was in Bromley's – Ritchie made light of it.

"That bloke won't check up on us – they're not his toys he's given us. Look – we got this plasticine set from Bromley's, didn't we? See this sticker on the back? Reduced to half-price. They only gave us the stuff they didn't want."

"I'll find out from my mum where that woman lives and we'll give her kids some of this. And if you know any kids, Ritchie…"

He seemed to have lost interest in the toys and just stared into space. Then he snapped out of his reverie and fished in his pocket for his ciggies.

"Shit," he said. "There aren't any left. I'll pop out and get some."

"OK," I said.

So then I was by myself. First I went over to the toys and tried to imagine how excited those kids would be when they got them. Then I looked round the room. Already it seemed to have absorbed Ritchie and me and it belonged to us. It was our HQ, I thought, and smiled. But I wished Ritchie would get back quickly. I was just a little jumpy, all by myself, and besides, I wanted him.

And it was at that point, when I was still coming down from our last exploit, when I was alone above the minicab office, waiting for Ritchie, that the truth hit me. I wanted him – and not just as a mate for getting kicks with. I admitted to myself that part of the glue that held us together was that I was a girl and he was a boy. I did fancy him. And what I wanted now was something to happen, but I didn't know what. You might think I was very naïve for a sixteen year old, and in some ways you'd be right. Only the reason I'd had little experience with lads is because I'd been waiting for the right one to come along – and now he had. Excitement tightened my throat and made my mouth dry. It was hard for me to swallow. Did he think in the same way about me? I wondered how I could find out.

I heard loud footsteps coming up the uncarpeted stairs. The door opened and there he was, with a white plastic carrier bag.

"Got us some provisions," he grinned.

He pulled out from the bag a party-size bag of crisps, a two-litre bottle of Coke and a bottle of vodka, along with some polystyrene cups.

"Where did you get the money from?" I asked him. But as my mouth formed the question, I knew the answer. People had been handing us money this evening right, left and centre. I watched Ritchie counting out notes.

"…fifty-five, sixty. Seventy, eighty, eighty-five… Yeah, eighty-five, and the rest of the change from the shop."

I swallowed hard. "What are we going to do with it?" I asked.

Ritchie shrugged. "We'll talk about it later. I'm parched." He opened the Coke and took a slug out of the bottle, then passed it to me. I drank some too. Ritch settled down on the floor, opened the crisps, lit up a cig and closed his eyes as he inhaled.

"I'll give up one day," he said.

I sat down by him, tearing the polythene cover off the tower of cups. I poured some Coke into each, but Ritch pointed to the vodka. I understood, opened that, and poured a shot into his Coke. Then I looked at my cup, and thought, what the hell, and put some in there too.

"This is good," Ritchie said.

His back was resting against the wall, his feet were on the floor, his knees bent. I was sitting by his side, my body echoing his. I knew I shouldn't have drunk that vodka. I wasn't used to it and it had made me flushed and headachy. Worse than that, I felt my control was slipping. But Ritchie seemed more relaxed than I'd ever seen him. And more talkative, too.

"Loz's brother is gonna open this place up again, when he's got some money together. What he's going to do, right, is sell old records – vinyl forty-fives and that. Collectors' items. You can make a bomb, going round car-boot sales, buying up things the owners don't know the value of. Like those early punk records. Car-boot sales are good places to unload whatever you've ended up with. Once me and Woodsy and Loz sold off a load of razors we'd nicked from the chemist. You get a good price for them."

"Razors?"

"Yeah, razors. There are mugs who'll buy anything. Go on, Anna, come up with a plan for getting us a load of stuff to flog at a car-boot sale."

He nudged me. I smiled.

"Not now," I said. My brain wasn't engaged. I was just trying to savour every minute of being here with Ritchie, making sure I imprinted each detail on my memory so I could think about it all later.

"You're good at making plans," he said. "And you've got nerve, too. I like that. You were cool as fuck in Bromley's."

"You too," I said. "When you came out with that business about having phoned the papers."

"It kills me," Ritchie said, "the way people fall over themselves to give to charity, but if you were really hard up and went to someone in the street to ask for money for yourself, they'd call you a beggar and spit at you."

I sort of edged closer to him. Our bodies were touching now but we were both looking straight ahead, not at each other. There was no way I was going to make the first move but I didn't know how to get him to do something. He was still talking, his voice becoming more emphatic. He was going on about the police now.

"They're just as bad, worse, in a way. It's all a game to them. They spend half their time chasing us when there are real villains out there. I mean, real villains. The ones that pay off the pigs, give them a bung. I know that happens, I know it for a fact. It all stinks."

"Hey, chill, Ritchie."

He stopped then, turned his face to me, and smiled. "You're not like them, Anna. You're the first decent person I've met."

My pulse was racing. My instinct told me not to say anything but just to look at him, keeping my gaze steady. It worked. With his finger he traced the outline of my face. His touch on my skin was electric. I was trembling all over, and tried to hide it. His finger rested for a moment on my lips. I saw a look of uncertainty in his eyes. Then he put his hand back by his side again.

"Ritchie," I said. My voice quivered. "It's OK. I want—"

And I stopped. Because there was someone downstairs, banging repeatedly on the wooden door. I was paralysed with fear. It was the police – it was the man from Bromley's – it was all of the toy-shop staff, who'd compared notes and were after us.

Swift as an arrow, Ritchie was out of the room and flying down the stairs. I found it impossible to get up – my legs wouldn't carry me. I knew they would find me there and I couldn't begin to think what I would say.

Then I heard Ritch shouting, swearing, but it was good natured swearing, and the other voices I heard were young, and I became pretty certain it was Loz, Tanner and Woodsy. My relief was mixed with annoyance. We weren't going to be alone any more. I noticed also I was completely sober again. The shock had brought me to my senses. But I knew something had changed permanently for me, and that something was how I felt about Ritchie.

They all came in, laughing, jostling each other, smelling a bit of cheap cider. Loz made straight for the toys and was trying to get a rise out of Ritchie, asking him what the hell he was doing stealing *toys*, for chrissake?

"That's not all we got," Ritch said, and took the wad of notes from his pocket. Tanner and Loz looked on, impressed. Meanwhile Woodsy saw the vodka. In a moment he'd unscrewed the top and downed a shot. He passed the bottle round. Ritchie was explaining what we'd been up to. I noticed he gave me a lot of credit, which was good.

"So Anna wrote this letter and printed it out, and got us these cards. And she goes in the shops with me, with her posh voice, and everyone's handing us money!"

The boys looked at me approvingly.

"You're all right for a bitch," Loz said.

That word shocked me, but only for a moment. I

realised it was just street talk, and a backhanded compliment, at that. Anyhow, I got my own back.

"You're pretty pathetic for a lad."

Woodsy laughed.

"And you're no better," I said.

Then Tanner explained to Loz and Woodsy how he'd helped us in the bookshop.

"Why didn't you let us in on that?" Loz asked Ritch.

"Because I didn't need you then. But we might be needing you all now." He shot a look at me, seeking my permission.

For a moment I was outraged. He should have consulted me first! But then I remembered we had kind of talked about a gang, and maybe Ritch was right – we could achieve even more if we had more people. I'd just make sure Ritch and I could still work together. So I nodded.

There was a change in the atmosphere at that point. Ritchie hoisted himself up on to the table and sat there, legs dangling. Tanner and Woodsy took the vodka and sat on the packing crates. Loz picked up a chair, turned it round and sat on it back to front, with his legs on either side of the chair back. I settled myself on the floor. Ritchie started talking, and we all listened.

"What's different about what we're doing – me and Anna – is that we think it all through. And we don't do over old ladies or people like us, cos that isn't fair. We've even given them what we've nicked – we're going to give those toys away. We don't just smash shop windows and that – we work out our plans in detail. Cause, like, the mugs who get caught, they're stupid. They make stupid mistakes. We don't."

"What you gonna do next?" Woodsy asked.

Ritchie looked at me. I really didn't know. It was too early to say. I just wanted to get shot of those toys and then I would think. It was a matter of coming up with someone who needed help, and someone who could afford to help them. I just said, "I'm working on it." I liked the way all the lads looked at me – the brains behind the outfit. But I felt the pressure to come up with something good.

"So what I wanna know," Tanner said, "is, do we give everything we nick to other people?" He sounded doubtful.

"Not *everything*," Ritchie said. "Obviously. So you can say now if there's anyone you wanna get, anyone who's got it coming to them."

I thought, that was the wrong way round, but I could see that Ritch didn't want to seem soft in front of his mates. It was funny, the closer I felt to him, the more I could understand things from his point of view, and see why he did things. From where he was sitting, right and wrong didn't count for much – it was more a matter of survival. His mates mattered to him, their opinion counted in a big way. And he needed to be in charge, because he felt safer that way. Like me. Which was why I was desperately trying to come up with a new scheme, even before we'd distributed our gains from the previous one. In the end it was Woodsy who started the ball rolling.

"My old man got the sack," he said. We all looked at him. "He had this job in a garage but the boss didn't need him any more, so he gave him the boot. He turned up for work a bit late on Monday and he told him to leg it. He didn't do nothing wrong, my dad."

Ritchie interrupted. "Yeah – and I bet his boss is loaded."

"Too right. He's got three garages and he drives a Merc. So I was thinking, like…" Woodsy looked at me.

I said, "Who would we give the money to?"

"Poor people," Loz interjected. "Oxfam. Whatever."

"Go on, Anna," Tanner said. "Think of something."

"I don't know enough about this guy," I said, floundering.

Woodsy carried on. "His name's Singh, Mr Singh." I saw Loz eye Ritchie – I wasn't sure why. "He's a real big shot. He's always going off to meetings."

"What sort of meetings?" I asked.

Woodsy looked blank, then grinned at me. "I remember my dad saying he belonged to some golf club in Redvale."

The golf club in Redvale. This was too much of a coincidence. Two nights ago Julia had rung my mother and asked if I'd be interested in a night's waitressing for the Redvale golf club's annual dinner dance. Despite the fact it was her, I'd agreed – I thought the money would come in useful. If ever there was proof we were right to do what we were doing, it was this coincidence. My mind zoomed into overdrive. If it was the annual dinner dance, this Mr Singh would probably be there. And if I was inside…

"Listen," I said. "I'm going to be waitressing at the golf club this weekend. I'll be inside – I can let you in. There's bound to be a cloakroom there, with coats and bags, and I could keep a lookout—"

"That's phat!" Woodsy said.

I glanced at Ritchie and our eyes met. It was brilliant – for a moment there was only me and him in that room. He was proud of me – I knew it. I was excited then and I started babbling. "It should be dead easy – I could have my mobile with me and text Ritchie. You'd have to be hanging around outside so you could get in quickly – but not together in case anyone suspected anything. We'd need a system of signals."

"We'll have another meeting," Ritchie said.

"Got any weed?" Woodsy asked.

It made me laugh, the way his attention had drifted. Woodsy struck me as the dimmest of the three of them.

Tanner was nice – I liked Tanner. Loz – well, even then, he frightened me a bit, to tell you the truth. Not because he looked evil or anything, but there was a blankness about him. I can't put it better than that.

Anyhow, the meeting sort of broke up. The vodka was passed around again, and Loz took a packet of something out of his pocket. I was hoping to ask Ritchie about arrangements for the morning – we still had to get rid of those toys. An uneasy thought passed through my mind. The shops might check that the hospitals and hospices had received the toys, and when they'd say they hadn't, they'd be on the look out for us. I went a bit cold at the thought, but it was just at that moment Ritchie's phone rang. He looked surprised, and answered it.

"Yeah… yeah. Yeah, I can. Outside Netto. OK."

He switched off his phone. "Sorry – gotta go." He threw Loz the key. And vanished.

The boys weren't bothered. They made themselves comfortable and didn't seem to mind that I was there. Tanner was quite drunk by now and passed me the vodka. But I wasn't going to stay. I asked if I could leave the toys overnight and said I was expected back home. Loz said, "No problem," and they all went, "See you around," in a friendly way, like I was one of them.

But I was troubled. Troubled about Ritchie. Why did he have to leave so quickly? Again I was reminded of the fact that there was so much about him I didn't know, or that he wasn't telling me. Yet something had happened between us tonight, I was sure of it. It would only be a matter of time before he opened up. If he would talk to anyone, it would be me. I recalled the feel of his finger on my skin. That had to mean something, didn't it?

So I went down the stairs and out into the street. My bus stop was at the crossroads, and the street was deserted. I felt a bit nervous being alone – you don't know the sort of characters who could be out at night. The crossroads was a pretty major junction. There was a big DIY emporium on one corner, and Netto on the other. Both were closed.

Ritchie had mentioned Netto, so my gaze roved over there – it was on the other side of the road to me. And there he was. I saw a girl – a blonde girl in a short, black-leather coat approach him, and kiss him on the cheek. She linked arms with him, and they walked off.

First I was numb. Then sick with betrayal. The funny thing was, the thing that really got to me, was that he'd given her his number, which was on the phone that *I'd* nicked for him. A wave of nausea hit me. But I had my pride. I wasn't going to follow him. Instead I made my way to my bus stop like there was nothing wrong, pretending – I was good at pretending, remember – and stood there, waiting for the ninety-seven, like a zombie. The walking dead. Other girls would have cried, but I don't do tears. I burn up inside instead, until only ashes are left.

CHAPTER TEN

I told myself I didn't care. I gave myself orders to carry on with my life. I got up in the morning, showered, had breakfast. Went to school, sat in my lessons, did the work, came home. Watched TV, had a bath, did some homework. I wouldn't let myself think. If you do – if you think about stuff – then it activates your emotions, and once they get going, you're lost.

The next day was just the same. I wasn't going to text Ritchie because I had my pride. I knew he wasn't going to text me. I wasn't going to go back to the room above the office to get the toys – the memories were too painful. They would stay there and I'd think about getting them another time. I wanted to get over Ritchie's betrayal first. I did allow myself to think that he hadn't betrayed me and maybe I'd betrayed myself by getting too involved with him. Either way, it was a mess.

I came back from school on Friday. I went upstairs, took off my school uniform and decided to have a shower. Mum was back at work part-time now and not doing too badly. I heard her come in just before I switched the shower on.

I shivered as the hot water made contact with my back and tensed myself as it cooled on contact with my body. I let the water run all over me, over all of my body, my hair, everywhere. Then I put some shower gel in my hands and rubbed it into a thick lather. It was one of Mum's – lavender for rest and relaxation with tea-tree oil for healing. I rubbed it in as hard as I could, getting rid of every possible speck of dirt or sweat or dead skin – who knows what accumulates during the day? I balanced one leg on the side of the bath tub and washed it vigorously. I reached to wash in between my toes – you perspire there, and the bacteria can smell. But the problem is, you put your shoes back on, and the bacteria are there, in your shoes, waiting to reinfect your toes. Which is why it's important to keep your feet clean. And there are other parts of you which keep producing sweat and stickiness.

I'd just finished rinsing my hair when I heard Mum shouting. I couldn't hear what she was saying as I had water in my ears. I reached for the towel, swept my hair up in it to make a turban and stepped out of the bath. She was outside the bathroom door now.

"Your mobile's ringing, Anna! I've got it here."

"Thanks," I said. I opened the bathroom door and extended a damp hand. She passed me the phone. It was still ringing madly. The display said it was Ritchie. I had to sit on the edge of the bathtub and take a deep breath before I picked up.

"Hi," I said, dead cool.

He sounded normal, as if nothing had happened. He said we needed to meet up to discuss the dinner dance tomorrow, said he'd been thinking about it and he'd had some ideas. Could I meet him later on in town?

I hesitated. I didn't know whether to tell him what I saw, but if I did, I would sound so pathetic, just like any normal girl. But we would have to talk. Maybe the best thing would be if we did meet, and then maybe, in a cool way, I could mention that I saw him with a girl. And then he would admit it, and I could see where I stood. If I wasn't happy, I'd pull out of the golf-club scam. Because I wasn't doing it without Ritchie.

So I said, yeah, all right, I'd meet him at nine in town. I took another towel and wrapped myself in it. When I came out of the bathroom, Mum was hanging about outside.

"Who's Ritchie?" she asked, smiling.

"A boy," I said, smiling too. I was feeling happier, see. I was going to meet him later.

"The same boy you told me about the other day?"

"Yeah, him. We're going out tonight. Just me and him. Maybe to see a film – I don't know yet."

"Is Ritchie his real name?"

"No. It's Craig."

Then my mum started fussing – what was I going to wear, was I going to have my hair up or down? I played along with her a bit, and promised I'd let her know how the evening went. I could always make up a suitable story later. Inventing was easy.

This is how to tell if someone's really got under your skin – that even if you're planning to have an awkward conversation with them, you're still looking forward to seeing them. All the way on the bus to town I could feel myself coming alive again. I even began to think about the golf-club dinner. Would there be a cloakroom attendant looking after the coats? Or security? I'd have to watch them, observe their movements, and calculate when the coast was clear. Even security guards are human – they pop outside for a fag, go to the gents. Maybe we ought to do some more play-acting. Ritchie could turn up in the role of my boyfriend, with a bunch of flowers, maybe, saying we'd had a tiff. Yeah. And I could seem upset, and all the while Tanner or someone could be going through the coats. Or perhaps he could pretend this Mr Singh had asked for his coat, and he could take it. Whatever. But it was hard to think of a role for the rest of the gang. They were better used getting rid of the loot afterwards. I didn't know if I could trust them on the scene.

The bus reached the bus station and I walked to The Broadway, where we'd arranged to meet, outside W H Smith. There was a bench facing it. I could see Ritchie was already there, hunched over his phone, either playing a game or texting *her*. I felt sick again.

But when he saw me he looked OK, not as if he'd been cheating on me. In fact, he seemed in a really good mood. I wondered why. We said hello and he asked me if everything was still on for tomorrow. I nodded. He didn't notice I was being quiet. He asked me if I could have a good look round the club premises where the dinner dance was being held, see what there was lying around, and who there was to tax. Tax. The use of that word tugged at me. It was *our* word. Then I realised I had a choice. I could sulk, act a bit off, until he asked me what was wrong, and then, bit by bit, giving him a mammoth guilt trip, I'd let him know. But that was game playing and not my style. I would take the other path.

"Ritchie. Who was that girl I saw you with outside Netto's?"

He looked completely baffled.

"On Thursday," I prompted him. "When you left us in Loz's brother's office."

He seemed genuinely confused. But was he acting? Since both of us had made a career out of being totally untrustworthy, could we trust each other?

Ritchie thought for a bit, and his face cleared. He smiled to himself. "Girl?" he questioned. "Come on. She's nearly forty."

An older woman? It was my turn to look baffled.

"That was Wendy," Ritchie explained.

"But," I spluttered. "But she looked... from the back... Why didn't you say you were meeting your mum?"

"What's it to you?" Ritchie teased.

I shrugged. I tried to play it cool but I knew he'd caught me out. Still, what did I care? Ritchie wasn't seeing another girl. Everything was back to the way it was before. I was drowning in a tidal wave of happiness. And there was even better to come.

"Wendy's been asking about you," Ritch said, matter-of-factly.

"Oh, has she?"

"Yeah. You can come to our place and meet her if you like. But you don't have to."

"No, I'd like to. I'd like to meet your mum."

"She can be a bit weird."

"All mums are weird," I half joked, thinking of mine.

"Anyway, I've got a surprise," he said. He grinned at me. Ritchie got up then and grabbed my hand. He dragged me off, and he was going so fast I had to run a bit to keep up with him. We came out of the other side of the precinct, emerging into some back streets. We catapulted round the corner and came to a stop in front of an old Nissan Micra.

"Fancy a drive?" he said.

I couldn't think what to say.

"Tanner's Dad let us have it. It's mine tonight. It's all right. The cops won't pick us up if I take it easy."

"Where did you learn to drive?"

"Around," he said. He took a key from his pocket and opened the passenger door. I slid in, feeling the springs give way. The seat needed fixing. The upholstery smelt a bit musty, a bit foul. I shuddered. But it was cool to have our own car and I could always have a good wash when I got home. Ritchie revved up, gunning the engine. I put on my seat belt, feeling good. This was what I liked best, taking a gamble, playing with fire.

Ritchie accelerated quickly and I felt myself pushed back against the seat. His driving was jerky but passable. I noticed he kept to thirty as we left the town centre, and stopped in time at all the lights. But once we were on the A road that led out of town, he picked up speed. I was a little frightened but I didn't say anything. There was a clunking noise from the back. He picked up a cassette tape then, and shoved it in the car's music system. Some garage blasted out. I didn't recognise it, but it was good. It kind of got into my bloodstream.

We didn't talk. Ritchie drove with fierce concentration. I didn't want to distract him, so I didn't ask where we were heading. After a while I recognised the outskirts of Fairfield. Ritchie slowed again, and I saw the community centre and the block of flats where I'd first met the other lads. Ritchie swung into an asphalt area at the foot of another, taller block of flats. He parked in front of a garage with no door, its interior full of junk.

We got out, and Ritchie locked up. Again he took me by the hand and led me to a lift. It was already at ground-floor level so in a moment we were lurched upwards. I wrinkled my nose at the smell. We got out at the floor below the top one. Within a moment or two Ritchie was unlocking one of the front doors along a narrow corridor that extended along the block. We entered.

It was pretty bare, except for the boxes lining the hall. It looked as if Ritchie and his mum hadn't done much unpacking, even though they'd been living in the flat for a few months. I noticed several doors leading off the corridor; Ritchie took me to the furthest one. He unlocked the door, and I followed him inside.

CHAPTER ELEVEN

His mum was sitting on a sofa, and it looked like she was doing a crossword. When we came in she turned, and looked surprised to see me. She rose, and questioned Ritchie with her eyes.

"This is Anna," he said. His voice was level.

Ritchie's mum – Wendy – made a big impression on me. It was hard to say why. To look at, she was nothing special. She was thin, blonde hair – dyed blonde, because you could see the roots. Face to face, she did look her age. Her complexion was sallow and there were lines on her forehead. She was wearing a V-necked sweater and the skin of her neck in the V-shape was red and rough. Her hipbones jutted out of the black leggings she was wearing. Scarlet-painted toenails peeped out from flowered mules. Like I said, on the surface she was like any of the women you'd see around Fairfield.

But there was something in her eyes.

"Hello, Anna," she said, with the trace of a Scottish accent.

"Hi," I said, uncomfortable about calling her Wendy yet.

She looked directly at me, summing me up. You could tell she was intelligent – you could see the way she was processing me. But when she'd done that, I saw what I thought was a tired, sad look in her eyes – even a dreamy look. You know, as if there was a big problem or something in her life. It made you want to ask her what was wrong. Because something was wrong, you could tell.

"It's nice to meet you," I said, determined to be polite and not knowing whether she was more shy than me. "Ritchie's spoken about you a lot."

"Has he, now? What has he told you?" Her voice wasn't jokey. Instead I got the impression she was referring to one specific thing that Ritch should have mentioned.

So I said, "Nothing." I glanced at Ritchie, who didn't meet my eyes. Instead he mooched over to a table and picked up a Game Boy. He started playing with it. He clearly didn't want to be part of this conversation.

"Has he told you why we're here?" she asked me.

"I know you moved here a few months ago. I met Ritch— Craig at St Tom's."

"Yes – he told me that. Thank you for being his friend. We need all the friends we can get."

In the background was a silly electronic tune from Ritchie's Game Boy. Ritchie's mum gestured to the sofa in an invitation to me to sit down. I did so, and she came to join me. I noticed then the faint white line of an ancient scar above her brow bone. I saw, too, that a muscle jumped in her cheek. Something about her scared me, and I'm not just saying this with hindsight.

"I'll tell you from the beginning, so you understand properly," Wendy said, pushing her hair back behind her ears. "I first met him eighteen years ago, when I was living in Greenock. That's where I come from, where my family comes from. Right from the start, Anna, there was something about us. That night we met in the pub, I singled him out. He singled me out. There was no one else in the room that night. We only had eyes for each other."

My mind was racing to make sense of this. Who was she talking about? Obviously not Ritchie. Ritchie's father? Her first love? Probably – because she was spouting all those romantic clichés – love across a crowded room, and so on. But what I didn't understand was why she was telling me all this. I mean, I'd only just met her. Was she all right in the head?

"We'd only been seeing each other for a fortnight when he asked me to live with him, but I knew, I knew it was going to happen from the off. These things are fated. Peter. Peter Duff. I call him Pete. He was a brickie. I gave up work because he was making so much that we didn't need my money. I cooked and cleaned, and I was completely content. I spent hours making myself look beautiful for him. Anna, you should have seen me then. He'd come home at night, and we couldn't keep our hands off each other."

I was getting more and more uncomfortable. And if *I* was uncomfortable, can you imagine how Ritchie was feeling? I glanced at him, but I couldn't even tell if he heard what his mother was saying. He was locked in another world with his Game Boy. It was like he was cutting himself off. I was alone.

"That was all I ever wanted, Anna, and I'm sure you'll agree it wasn't a lot. I just wanted to look after the man of my dreams. It's all any woman ever wants. But he was a weak man, Anna. He was led astray. He started to want to go out. At first, he told me it was just to drink with his mates. But I heard rumours that he'd been with other women. When I asked him about the rumours, he denied them, of course. It made him angry and he lost his temper. I was sore after that beating, I can tell you, aching in every bone. But we made up. It was better than ever."

Wendy's eyes were locked in the distance, and I felt as if she was reliving her past.

"You see, Anna, he really loved me. He never meant to hurt me. Sometimes I lost my temper with him, too. We knew how to fight – it was because we loved each other so much."

Her face darkened now. She took my hand and gripped it hard.

"That was when we conceived Craig. The day I told him the news, he'd been drinking. He was in a temper and he shouted, he said Craig wasn't his. He accused me of having other lovers. Anna. I've never slept with another man except for Craig's father. You believe me, don't you? And then Peter kicked me out. I ended up in a bed and breakfast. But I didn't give up. I was determined to get my man back. Pete was my baby's father. I called him every day. And then he moved. I followed him. And then... Craig? I forget what happened next."

She looked over at Ritchie. Obviously he had been listening because he supplied the answer.

"You weren't well. You were in hospital."

"I was in hospital," Wendy repeated. "Then I went to another hospital and had the baby and they wouldn't let me have him at first. So I got myself better. And I worked at nights. I tried to make a new start and we moved to Sheffield. I met Bill in Sheffield. We lived with him for a while, but it didn't work out. I'm the kind of woman, Anna, who only loves once – and for ever. But I wasn't ill again. I can control myself, and I will control myself, for Craig's sake. I hope I've been a good mother. But the lad needs a father. I'm sure that's why he's got in with the wrong crowd. I do my best for him, Anna. I look after his education. I buy him books."

She pointed to a unit full of paperbacks. It was an incongruous detail in the otherwise bare room.

"Then at the end of last year I was on the bus and I saw a van, and on the side it said, *Peter Duff, Builder*. A white, modern van. Peter Duff, it said. And a telephone number. I memorised it, Anna. I learnt it off by heart. I went straight home and I rang the number. 'Is that Peter Duff, the builder?' I asked. A woman's voice said it was. 'Can you give me your full postal address?' I asked. The fool did. It's just five miles from here. That night I said to Craig, we're moving here. I want to give it one last shot."

I just nodded. There was nothing I could say. She was in the grip of an obsession.

"I made sure Craig got in to a good school. I care about him, Anna. He's all I've got. I started work as a barmaid. I've pulled pints in more pubs than you've had hot dinners. Then after a few weeks, when I was ready, I took a trip to Pete's yard. He's done well for himself, bloody well. There was a BMW in the yard, it's his. I saw him leave his office and get into it." She squeezed my hand tight. "He looks older, Anna, but he hasn't changed. He's still my Pete. He has a new family now, and I'm not saying I want to spilt them up. I would never do that. There are children, you see. But I just want to talk to him one last time, Anna. He's got to meet Craig. He has to admit that Craig is his son. Look."

She got up from the sofa and was soon scrabbling around in a cupboard, then brought out a newspaper cutting. She thrust it at me. It was one of those pictures where a person is handing over one of those huge cheques to a charity. The person receiving it was a woman; the person handing it over was the dead spit of Ritchie. The caption identified him as Peter Duff, local builder and property developer.

"They do look alike," I said.

"All I want him to do is acknowledge his son," Wendy said. "Is that a lot to ask? I want them to meet. Craig is a clever lad. He'll go far. He should go to university. He needs money. Peter's never given us a penny in all these years. I've struggled alone. Not that I mind, I love my son more than life itself. I do, Anna. Which is why I'd do anything for him. There's no escaping your destiny. I knew it the night I met Pete. It was in the pub. I was there with a friend—"

She'd reached the end and was about to start again at the beginning. I reckoned her drama with Ritchie's dad replayed itself constantly.

Ritchie cut in at that point. "Do you want a cup of tea, Wendy?"

She started at the sound of his voice. "No, I've just had one. Sorry, Anna, I know I do go on. But these things eat away at you. Craig, put the kettle on for Anna."

"It's all right, Mrs Ritchie," I said. "I've got to go home now. My mother's expecting me."

"I'll take you home," Ritchie said.

"That's a good lad," Wendy commented.

So it was relatively easy to get out. We all said our goodbyes and in a few moments Ritch and I were standing by the lift.

"She's not well," Ritchie muttered.

"She seems, like, a bit obsessed?" I hesitated. It's hard, talking to someone about their mother.

"Yeah, well, it hasn't been easy for her. He left her without a penny. It's not fair. So sometimes she gets a bit…"

"Yeah," I acknowledged.

"She just…" Ritchie's voice trailed away again.

Have you ever had a conversation like that? When the words you say are rubbish, but actually you're reading someone's mind. Ritchie was trying to tell me that he was embarrassed by his mum, but also that he felt sorry for her. That he felt he should look after her, but also that he was out of his depth. I was honoured that he introduced us and trusted me to pick up the situation, and I wanted him to know I understood. Our silence conveyed all that, I think. Then I said to him, "It must be hard for you."

"No," he said. "I manage. Listen, Anna, forget about all this. Let's go somewhere. We've got the motor. Let's drive somewhere."

"OK," I said.

The lift came then, and within a few moments we were downstairs, outside, and back at the car. Next thing, we were flying along the road. There wasn't too much traffic and we were doing about sixty. It was like we were leaving Wendy and the flat miles and miles behind. I sensed Ritchie's relief. As for me, I was loving seeing the trees, hedges and houses whizz past, a blurred backdrop to us: me and Ritch. I wanted to forget about Wendy too. Ritchie steadied the car to a safer speed as the road narrowed and we got out into the country. The tape came to an end and he didn't turn it over.

"When I get back," he said, "Wendy's going to ask me whether we're going out together."

That was the first time he'd mentioned anything like that. I felt stupidly happy.

"Are we?" I questioned him.

"It's up to you," he said.

That wasn't good enough. "Do you want to go out with me?" I prodded.

"Yeah," he said, sort of nonchalantly.

"I want to go out with you too."

We drove on a little more, not saying anything. Then Ritchie pulled into a car park adjoining a pub, The Swan with Two Necks. We got out, walked to the wall at the end of the car park, and vaulted over it. We scrabbled our way down a grassy bank to a clump of trees. It was almost pitch black. It took my eyes time to get adjusted to the dark. We settled down on the ground, underneath a large tree. It was cold – we huddled up. I could hear the occasional car rush past and a faint buzz from some nearby electricity pylons. I knew what would happen next. He kissed me.

You'll believe this because you know I'm not soft. It was the most amazing kiss ever. It seemed to travel all through me, getting to every bit of my body. When I'd pulled blokes before it was just for show, to prove I could do it. Kissing Ritchie was different. It was partly the physical thing of being so close to him, but also I was getting to know him. I could feel he was hesitant but turned on, it was like he was telling me secret things, but without language. All that from the way our mouths met and got all mixed up.

We didn't do anything else except for kiss, not then. People looking over the wall could have seen us and, anyway, it was too cold. Ritch had his parka on and I was wearing a coat with a fur-lined hood. I remember the biting air and snuggling up to Ritchie, wanting his body's warmth, wanting to give him mine.

I forget how long it was, but Ritchie broke away to light a cigarette. The flame of his lighter was a tiny beacon. I heard him inhale deeply to get the cigarette going.

"You're my girl now," he said.

I couldn't let him get away with that. "And you're my bloke." We were equal, remember.

"In the beginning I didn't fancy you," Ritchie said, sort of thinking aloud. "Not in your school uniform.

Maybe I wouldn't have noticed you if you hadn't come up to talk to me. But you did, and I appreciated that. I was gutted when it turned out to be you I tried to mug. Sorry," he said.

"Don't mention it."

"I don't know when I first started fancying you. Maybe when you nicked those shoes. I saw you in a different light then. You surprised me – you weren't what I expected. You're tough – you're not like the other girls I know, they're just slags. Well, they can't help it, half of them. I never thought I'd have a girlfriend, not until after my mum sorted herself out. But I don't reckon that'll ever happen."

There was something I wanted to know. "Is she going to confront your dad? It sounded like she was pretty serious."

"Yeah. She's got hold of his address. I don't think he'll agree to see her. She wants to take me there."

"Isn't that a bit risky?"

"What do you mean, risky?"

"I don't know. He might call the police or something."

"Whatever."

"Do you want to go, Ritchie? Do you want to meet your dad?"

"No. He's a bastard. I hate his guts. But Wendy wants me to see him, and it might shut her up. What I'm thinking is, if he admits he's my dad, she'll give the whole thing a rest. Either he'll give us some money, or she'll be so blazing angry she won't want to see him again."

I chuckled to myself. "My mum would call that 'achieving closure'."

"You what?"

"Like, giving the whole thing a proper ending. So you can move on. My mum's into all that therapy stuff. She's as crazy as your mum." I said that to make Ritchie feel better, but as I said it, I knew it wasn't true. My mum felt sorry for herself sometimes, but she still had a grip on reality. Ritchie's mum scared me.

Ritchie was silent for a bit. I thought to myself, whatever happens, I'd stand by him. I decided that he needed me, and I wasn't going to let him down. I didn't need words to tell him that. I pulled him to me and kissed him again.

We stayed there until the dampness in the ground seemed to travel up and through us. Reluctantly we got up and went back to the car park. Neither of us wanted to talk about Wendy and her plans. But we didn't have to. We had other things to preoccupy us. We were taxers. We needed to plan what was going to happen at the dinner dance. Ritchie reckoned I'd be able to open a window somewhere and let one of the lads in – Tanner was small, he could squeeze in anywhere. And maybe there was a trophy lying around which could bring in a bit of cash. I said Ritch could come to see me, pretend to be my brother, and then I could pass him anything I'd lifted. Though it was hard to plan, not having ever been inside the clubhouse before. There was a risk attached, I knew. But I liked risks.

Ritchie took me all the way home. It must have been nearly one in the morning when we got back. It was hard to part. Once in bed, I thought through all the stuff Wendy had told me and wondered what Ritchie's childhood must have been like. It was almost impossible to imagine. All I knew was, I felt sorry for him. I rolled my duvet up, and hugged it, wanting it to be Ritchie. And so I fell asleep.

CHAPTER TWELVE

We swung into the drive leading to the golf club, Mum and me. There were trees on either side, and then the drive turned and led down the side of the long, low building where the car park was. I got a good view of the surrounding land. I noticed that the car park was large and sloped down on the right to a border of shrubs and bushes. On the left I could see the dim outline of what I imagined was the golf course, adjoining the clubhouse. There was a van parked next to the kitchen with men unloading things.

"I wish you'd have changed before you left home," Mum said. "I'd have liked to have seen you in your waitress uniform."

"Looking such a dork," I finished. "There is no way I'm going to risk having any of my mates see me dressed up like a French maid."

"I'd think you look rather sweet."

I just laughed. At my feet was my sports bag, with a black skirt, white shirt, my black school shoes and black tights. And room in it for whatever I could find on the premises.

I gave my mum a peck on the cheek and said I'd give her a bell when I knew what time I was finishing. Then I made my way to the kitchen.

You know, it's funny. They say that crime doesn't pay and yet one thing I'd got from Ritchie's and my exploits, was increased confidence. A few months ago I would have been nervous, having to be a waitress. Now I knew how to act, how to put on a front. I could do anything. My nerves were reserved for hoping our plans would go without a hitch.

I entered the kitchen and made myself known to the people there and they introduced me to Donna, the head waitress. She seemed nice. She was a big, rather lumpy woman, her hair in a bun, and glasses perched on her nose. She told me she couldn't wear her contact lenses as they were making her eyes sore. I explained I needed to get changed and so she pointed to the ladies.

To get there I needed to cross the room where the dinner was being held. It was a smallish hall. There were ten or so round tables which were in the process of being prepared by a group of waiters and waitresses, most looking a little older than me. In one corner was a raised platform with some musical equipment. There was a space around it. When I came out of the hall I found myself in the lobby. There were a number of doors but the ladies was clearly marked. And immediately I saw what I was looking for. Between the ladies and the gents was a small room with the door ajar. In it were two moveable units for hanging coats on. Already there were some jackets there. I filled with exultation. Our plan was going to work. Because the room didn't have space for an assistant, the coats would just be left there and, best of all, there was a window at the far end, a dirty-looking window, big enough for someone to climb through. I walked over to it to check it wasn't locked. As far as I could see, it was just an ordinary sash window. I darted back to the cloakroom door, pushed it almost shut, ran back to the window and lifted it a couple of inches. That was our sign. Now they would know which one was the cloakroom window, and they would also know it would be OK to follow our plan.

Then I went next door to the ladies, took my bag into a cubicle and texted Ritchie. I told him about the window and reminded him of our signal for the all clear. I got changed, and just as I was wriggling into my skirt, he texted back. All of them were in the Micra round the corner. It was looking good. Ritchie reckoned they needed the car. He said they'd look more suspicious approaching the clubhouse on foot, and they needed to make a quick getaway.

Outside the cubicles there was a mirror and I checked my appearance. I redid my hair, scraping it right back in a ponytail. I was wearing just a little bit of make-up, because I wanted to look slightly older and responsible. And there was another reason too. Because of Ritchie. I know that was so stupid of me as he'd seen me loads of times without make-up, but now it was different. Now it was important that he kept on fancying me. I didn't want to lose what I valued so highly.

I could feel my stomach knotting. That familiar feeling was kicking in – the mixture of dread and excitement. I reviewed our plans. I had to find out where the trophies were kept. If it was possible, I was going to lift one and put it in my sports bag. Ritchie would turn up and I'd give him the bag. Since his arrival would create a diversion, that would be the moment when one of the lads would get in through the window and go through the coats. We'd decided to assume that one of the coats would belong to that Mr Singh. Of course, there was a chance he wouldn't be there, but somehow I knew he would. Things always worked out for me and Ritchie.

This was the first time, though, we'd planned to steal from real people – I mean, as opposed to shops. The way I thought about it was, these people could afford it. I didn't know much about golf or golf clubs, but I did know you have to be reasonably rich to join one. Anyway, they were all probably insured. When they got home and realised their credit cards or whatever were gone, they'd ring their banks and stop them. All they'd lose was some cash and a few bits and pieces. It was no big deal. Most of it would find its way to Oxfam. I had a guilty pang then about the toys that were still lying in the office, but I thought maybe it was better they should stay there, until the heat was off.

When you think about it, why should some people be rich, and others poor? I remembered the way Ritchie's mum lived and what she said about Ritchie's dad having a BMW. Where was the justice in that? And by the sound of it, this Mr Singh exploited people. I thought about all those celebrities who earn millions of pounds for just prancing about on the stage or on a catwalk, and how they get so up themselves. I smiled. Maybe it was doing rich people a favour to relieve them of their money. You could have too much, couldn't you?

So I left the ladies just as another girl dressed in waitress uniform was coming in. She smiled shyly at me and introduced herself as Kelly. I was glad people were being friendly.

Back in the kitchen Donna explained what was expected of us. We had to help lay the tables. Then we had to go back to the kitchen and we would be given trays of hors d'oeuvres to pass round, once people had started to arrive. Then we just had to bring out the food to the tables, and clear away the old plates. Finally we had to serve coffee. And then we were free to go. I was going to earn thirty quid doing that. I decided I might give some of it to Ritchie.

*   *   *

My tray had little mushroom vol-au-vents, cocktail sausages on sticks and tiny pastries that Donna said had a cheesy filling. I walked out of the kitchen and into the dining hall, where quite a few people had congregated. There was a string quartet now, playing something or other. All the women wore long, flashy dresses. The men were in suits. I saw Mr Singh straightaway. He was the only Sikh there. Sikh men always wear turbans because they're not allowed to cut their hair. He was a tall, fat man, wearing an expensive-looking suit and a scarlet tie. He was in the centre of a knot of people all talking and laughing. I took my tray in his direction.

When the people saw me they all began to help themselves. I had a grin plastered to my face. Mr Singh's eyes met mine and he smiled. It was a friendly smile and for a moment I felt a bit bad. But I remembered what Woodsy had said. This man had sacked his dad. I mustn't be led astray by appearances. Mr Singh was probably ruthless in his business life.

My tray was soon empty and I returned to the kitchen to get another. Some people helped themselves without acknowledging me at all, others smiled and even said thank you. When Julia recognised me she squealed and waved. I felt myself blush. I prayed she wouldn't come over and kiss me or anything. Partly because that would be so embarrassing and partly because it was vital I didn't draw attention to myself. Complete anonymity was the best cover. Luckily Julia was all over some man, flirting like crazy. Walking to and from the kitchen I began to wonder when I would get a chance to find out where the trophies were.

Donna said they were ready now to sit down for the first course, and a few of us stood by the kitchen door watching the guests go to their tables. I kept my eye on Mr Singh. Accompanied by a petite Indian lady, he made his way to a table in the centre of the room – then I went white with horror. Sitting there already was someone I recognised – it was the manager from the toy shop, Bromley and Bromley, the one who had questioned us. He would be bound to recognise me. I couldn't possibly serve that table. For a second I just wanted to run and abandon the whole thing.

Then I pulled myself together. Anna, I said, think of Ritchie. He likes you for your nerve. Stay calm. I looked over at Mr Singh's table again. I stared hard. The chances were that I could arrange to be attached to another table. Everything was going to be fine.

We were told to get back in the kitchen and wait for the signal from Donna to fetch the empties from the first course. Then someone told me I was table number seven. There was no time, or reason, to raise an objection. I prayed that seven was not Mr Singh's table.

But as I went into the hall with the other waiters and waitresses, my eyes locked on to him, and in the middle of his table was a card with the figure seven. It partly obscured the face of the manager from Bromley's. I walked out into the hall and took a deep breath. I made my feet take me in that direction. I reached the table. I couldn't help but sneak a glance at the toy-shop manager. I looked again. It wasn't him! It was another man – a shorter one, with a faint, thin moustache. I had been imagining things. I couldn't understand how I could have possibly mistaken this man for the guy from Bromley's. I filled with relief which expressed itself in a radiant smile.

"Good evening," Mr Singh said to me. "Are you our waitress for the evening?"

"I think so," I said.

He grinned, and nodded at me. "Now, remember, young lady," he said. "I've got quite an appetite!" His wife laughed at him. There was a friendly atmosphere on the table, and it seemed to emanate from Mr Singh. Appearances can be deceptive.

For the next fifteen minutes or so I was frantically busy, going to and from the kitchen, bringing plates, vegetarian alternatives, potatoes, vegetables, refilling jugs of water, and quite enjoying being so busy. It was so much easier to be doing things rather than waiting around, thinking about what was going to happen later.

And it was to be sooner rather than later, as once I'd returned with an empty jug of water, Donna said we could have a twenty-minute break before the next course. There was some food for us if we wanted it.

Food was the last thing on my mind. I realised this was the moment. While all the guests were eating, it was unlikely there would be anyone around near the cloakroom. So I excused myself and went out to the ladies. The game was beginning.

Once in the lobby, I decided to try all the doors. One said "Office". It was locked. The next I tried opened easily. It looked like some kind of conference room. There was a long table in the middle with chairs all around. And there, against the wall, was the trophy cabinet. I stood there, summoning my resolve. I knew it might be locked, but there was a chance it wasn't. As quickly as possible, I had to open it, remove one or two items, dart into the cloakroom where my sports bag was, and put them in.

But what seemed so easy when I was planning it with Ritchie seemed almost impossible now. Wrong, even. I desperately wished he was with me. Then it wouldn't have even mattered if we were caught. I wanted to be doing the same thing as him. Then I told myself he'd be with me in a few minutes. I thought about how pleased he'd be if I'd managed to lift a trophy or two.

I had enough presence of mind not to switch the light on. But I knew if I closed the door it would be so dark I wouldn't be able to see what I was doing. So I risked leaving the door slightly open. I walked over to the cabinet.

"Hello, young lady! What are you doing in here?"

I recognised the voice. It was Mr Singh. I froze in terror. My mind raced – how was I going to get out of this? I prayed for inspiration and it came.

"I wasn't feeling too good," I lied.

"What's wrong?" He sounded concerned.

"I've got a migraine. I suffer from them. I just thought if I could sit in a dark room for a few minutes, while my pills take effect…"

"Can I do anything for you? Would you like me to fetch you a glass of water? Shall I let someone know you're not feeling well?

"No – it's all right." I forced a smile. "I want to last out the evening. I need the money."

"Oh, no! Don't let that stop you going home. I'll square it with the caterers and make sure you get full wages. You've worked hard enough already."

"No – I want to stay. I will feel better, when the pills take effect. I'm used to this, honestly."

"Are you sure?"

"Yes, really."

"Well, have a word with my wife later. She's a medical lady."

He left me then. I had to sit down because my legs

couldn't carry me a moment longer. I had never been so near being discovered. But it was OK. I was safe. I knew I couldn't possibly break open the trophy cabinet now, but it wasn't the end of the world. I would ring Ritchie and tell him to come anyway. The second part of our plan would still work.

My fear was now affecting my stomach and I had to go to the ladies for real. The room was empty, apart from the whiff of mingled perfumes from the female guests. I went into the same end cubicle I was in before. Sitting there, something caught my eye. An earring. A gold drop earring. When I had finished, I picked it up. That would be worth a bob or two. I cheered up instantly. I would have something to give Ritchie. I'd had a close shave. Luck was still with us. I rang Ritchie's mobile.

Within a few moments the buzzer was ringing at the front door that led into the lobby. I was there so I opened it. There was Ritchie. As soon as I saw his face, I felt better. I was about to explain what had happened when I heard the sound of people behind me. But that wasn't a problem. We had this all worked out. I turned, and it was Kelly and another girl.

"Oh, hi. This is my brother, Craig."

"Hi, Craig," Kelly said. I didn't like that flirty edge to her voice. But I could hardly challenge it, now I'd said he was my brother.

"Yeah," Ritchie drawled. "I need the house keys. I called in, in case you've got them. I'll take your bag back if you like, as I've got the car."

"Do you drive?" asked Kelly. "What do you drive?"

"An Audi TT."

"Ooh!" she replied.

"Craig – I need to speak to you," I said. He heard the urgency in my voice and followed me into the trophy room. I explained very quickly what had happened, then passed him the earring. He said it was probably nine-carat gold and I was pleased. He said never mind about the trophy. I could tell he was edgy, not his usual self, but I guess it was the pressure of the job. I didn't feel too great myself. Both of us knew that at this moment in time Woodsy or Tanner was going through the coats.

We emerged back into the lobby and – guess what? – Kelly was still there. She spoke directly to Ritchie.

"Are you older than Anna, then, to be able to drive?"

"Yeah, I'm eighteen."

"Cool. Do you work or what?"

"I'm a cocktail waiter," Ritchie said, slick as anything. I was a bit annoyed at Kelly, but enjoying Ritchie's lies, too.

"Where? In town?"

I knew what she was up to. She wanted to find out where he worked, and then she'd be round there, chatting him up. So I waited with amusement to hear what Ritchie would say. That was when Julia materialised.

"Anna darling! You've been working so hard – I shall tell your mother what a treasure you are. Hello – who's this?"

Oh my God. I couldn't pretend that Ritchie was my brother any longer. Panic gripped me.

"My boyfriend," I said in a small voice. Julia's eyes lit with interest.

"Now I remember your mother saying something about a new man in your life. Aha! So you can't keep away, can you?" she said to Ritchie, giving him a good once-over. Then she disappeared into the ladies.

"What?" Kelly said. "You said he was your brother? Which are you?"

Ritchie looked at me quizzically. I shot him a look as if to say, leave me to handle this.

"He's my boyfriend. We were just kidding."

She wasn't too pleased. "You're weird, you," she said, and went into the ladies too. That gave Ritchie and me another moment alone together. He said he reckoned Woodsy should have been in and out by now. The cloakroom door had been closed throughout. I'd made sure of that. I realised I hadn't given Ritchie my bag, but now I didn't need to, and I couldn't have anyway, as it was in the cloakroom. Everything was getting awkward and complicated and I could hardly keep everything in my mind at the same time. It flashed across my mind that more than anything I wanted to be out of here and somewhere with Ritchie – back in the country again, anywhere. He kissed me briefly on the lips and went. He said he'd stay in close touch.

After he'd gone, first Julia and then Kelly and her friend had emerged from the ladies and gone back to the dinner. I was on my own again. Curiosity overpowered me. I opened the cloakroom door to see what damage Woodsy had done. He had been very clever. The room and coats looked untouched. The window had been replaced exactly as I'd left it. In fact it looked as if no one had been in. I paused. *Had* he been in? Had something else gone wrong?

I knew I couldn't loiter, so I closed the door again and went back to the kitchen to help serve dessert. There was a choice – fruit salad or chocolate bombes. I made my way to Table Seven carrying two bombes.

"Ah! Our waitress!" said Mr Singh. "Are you feeling better?"

"Yes – much," I lied.

"Allow me to introduce my wife. She's a doctor. Our waitress suffers from migraines. What would you suggest?"

His wife laughed. "I'm not a GP," she explained to me. "I specialise in pain relief."

"She works at the hospice," said Mr Singh proudly, digging into his bombe.

"Mmm. Delicious. I hope they save one for you," he grinned at me. "Although chocolate can trigger migraines. I was going to ask you – can you ask the other waiters if anyone has seen a gold earring. Mrs Hartley –" he gestured to a lady across the table "– has lost one. It was a gift from her mother. She'll be so glad if it turns up."

"OK, I will," I said, returning to the kitchen.

Well. It was too late, I thought. Ritchie already has the earring. It won't appear now. I told myself there was no point being upset about it. But – I'll admit this now – I was upset. It was different, knowing who you've taxed. I felt mean. And, Mr Singh was being so nice to me. I began to wonder if maybe Woodsy's dad had deserved the sack for some reason. There are two sides to every story. I was more confused than ever, and the headache I'd lied about earlier was becoming a reality. Then I remembered that it was OK. Apart from the earring, we'd taken nothing. By all appearances Woodsy had not been in the cloakroom, and we could write the whole evening off as a bad experience, no harm done. And I could even suggest to Ritchie that we could post the earring back to the golf club – it couldn't possibly be worth that much by itself. Then we could just go back to taxing shopkeepers.

All this was going through my mind as I was pouring coffee. Table Seven had relaxed now and they were asking me about myself. They'd learned I was still at school and what GCSEs I was taking, and that I knew Julia. Mrs Singh offered me a petit four, and I declined, but liked the way they were drawing me in to their world. Now I was positively grateful that Woodsy had failed.

We cleared away the coffee things, and as we were doing that some people began to move the tables to one side for the dancing. I knew that I'd be free to go then. I thought I'd text Ritchie before I rang my mum. I hoped we could snatch some time together. It might even be possible for him to run me home instead – it would save Mum a journey. The idea of having some time alone with him blotted out all the mishaps of the evening.

So I wasn't one of the first to leave. I stayed in the kitchen to send that text to Ritchie. Other waiters and waitresses got their coats and went out the door that led directly to the car park. I started to press the letters on my phone. Then one of the waiters came back in.

"Some idiot's broken into my car!" he was shouting. Everyone looked over at him. Then another woman came back. "I can't get into my car," she said. "The lock's been ruined."

I don't remember the sequence of what happened next, sorry. But other people went to check the car park, and nearly every car had been interfered with. Radios were gone, locks damaged, stuff taken. Someone was ringing for the police. The news filtered through to the guests who were dancing, and the festivities stopped. Everyone was outside checking their cars. Then Mr Singh came back in, and announced, his face creased in puzzlement, "My car's gone."

I read in the newspapers they found it the next day, smashed up, abandoned in a ditch, with *Paki bastard* spray-painted across the windscreen.

CHAPTER THIRTEEN

The problem with baths is that you can never be sure you're really getting clean. Because the old water circulates, it doesn't go anywhere. You scrub yourself with soap but all the bits that come off with the soap stay in the water. The water goes murky with them. And if the bath is too hot, and you begin to sweat, where does the sweat go? It stays in the water and might come back and cling to you. But on the other hand, you can be certain in a bath that the water is reaching every bit of you. But now you understand why I shower both before and after a bath. I mean, it makes sense, doesn't it?

I was in the bath on the Sunday night after the event at the golf club. It was a good place to think. I'd had one brief text message from Ritchie. *Sorry*, it read. That was early Sunday morning, about three o'clock. When I read it, I knew immediately what must have happened. Raiding the cars and trashing Mr Singh's Merc was the gang's idea. Ritchie was powerless to stop them.

In which case, why hadn't he replied to any of my texts? Maybe he was lying low, until the heat was off. Perhaps his phone was switched off, or he lent it to his mum or something. I hated having to wait around like this. It was horrible, bottling up everything I felt.

I'd decided I wasn't going to think about any of what happened on Saturday night until I was with Ritchie. Replaying it in my mind would drive me mad. There was no point. Analysing your feelings is the kind of pathetic thing my mum would do.

But I couldn't stop the pictures in my head. White, distraught faces. Donna, the head waitress, sobbing, because she didn't know how she was going to be able to get her car fixed. Mr Singh striding back into the hall, saying his car had gone. And the question he asked: "What have I done wrong?" The policewoman who came into the kitchen looking so concerned, saying we were free to go.

My mum had wanted to know all about it on the way home. Then in the morning Julia had rung with the news about the Merc. She said they were treating it as a race-hate crime. Mum said people who do that sort of thing are the scum of the earth, lower than animals. To attack someone because they are a different race or religion was stupid and ugly. She got quite worked up.

I just concentrated on acting like normal. I had to protect Ritchie, which you'll agree was reasonable, because I was pretty certain he wouldn't have done such a thing. I did notice that Mum's anger made her come out of herself a bit. In the past few weeks she'd been getting back to normal. And Julia had persuaded her to part with some of her hard-earned cash to go away for a weekend for a massage course. It gave me a jolt to realise how quickly that weekend had come around – it was next Saturday, in fact. I had insisted to Mum I didn't mind her going away, and it was true. I quite like having the house to myself. But for some reason, right now, I wished she wasn't going. I just wanted her to be around. Just around.

Whenever I did think about Saturday night, I controlled my thoughts by saying:

1) *I* didn't do anything;

2) Ritchie probably didn't do anything;

3) The gang was after Mr Singh anyway and there was probably little I could have done to prevent it.

Then I would think about something else. I made myself. I had to.

I was glad to go to school on Monday because I could concentrate on my lessons. There was a big debate in the formroom about whether Janette had lost her virginity. I smiled but didn't join in. She'd been going out with a twenty-year-old bloke, so everyone thought they were sleeping together. There was a science test later so some people were testing each other, or cramming as much in as possible alone at their desks.

It was English next, *Macbeth* again. Everyone was moaning because they all hate Shakespeare. So the teacher was really trying hard, trying to make it exciting. She was going on about how Macbeth ordered the killing of Macduff's wife and children, and how brutally it was carried out. She read out the scene with Macduff hearing the news, and how he couldn't take it all in. Her voice was breaking. Then she said it showed how evil Macbeth was, to arrange the killings of innocents.

I said how did she know Macbeth ordered it? She said because he was after Macduff. But I said, it doesn't say anywhere in the play that Macbeth wanted the wife and children killed. Maybe the murderers took it on themselves to do the killings without permission, because *they* were the evil ones. Maybe Macbeth would be shocked when he found out what happened.

The teacher said, "Technically you could be right, Anna. But I think it's unlikely, don't you? Macbeth had got used to killing, used to blood. By that stage in the play he was only thinking of himself."

"No, Miss," I said. "What about Lady Macbeth – he was thinking of her too."

"You have a point. But what Shakespeare is trying to say is that evil breeds evil."

"But it was an accident," I said.

The teacher looked puzzled. I noticed my hands were dirty and made a note to go and wash them at the end of the lesson.

In Maths I felt my phone vibrate in my blazer pocket. When the teacher was writing on the board I checked it.

Ritchie. He wanted to meet me in the afternoon. Four thirty. At Moor Park gates. At last.

I'd had time to go home first and get changed into my jeans and a fleece. Ritchie was waiting for me. I saw him before he saw me. He was just stubbing out a cig. When he looked up, there I was.

"You all right?" he asked me, smiling.

I smiled back. It was just so good to be back with him again, and I realised how much I'd missed him.

"Yeah," I said. It just bowled me over, how good-looking he was. I know it sounds silly, that I'd known him so long and didn't see that in the beginning. But there's a kind of beauty about him. His eyes are greyish-brown. When he smiles, it's as if he's trying not to smile, but can't help it. His hair had grown quickly and it covered his scalp like dark fur. I wanted to reach out and stroke it. Instead I linked arms with him and we walked into the park. We were unremarkable, just any boy and girl.

"Let me tell you what happened on Saturday night," he said.

"OK."

"After I saw you, I went back out to where we'd parked the Micra and there was Tanner throwing up in the bushes. I don't know whether the drink had disagreed with him, or what. But I reckoned he was the only one small enough to get in through the window. Loz got really irate then, cursing and that. It was Woodsy's idea to get the Merc, cos he said he'd be able to recognise it."

"Mr Singh was all right, Ritch. He was nice to me."

Ritchie threw me a sidelong glance, then carried on with his narrative. "There was some gear in the back of the Micra, spanners, cans of paint. Loz knows how to spray the CCTVs so they can't operate. Anyway, he and Woodsy were at the cars then. Loz knows what to do because of his brother. So when they'd got a couple of radios and some bits and pieces, Woodsy found the Merc. There was no alarm or anything, so it was easy. Woodsy and Loz drove away in it, and I got Tanner up from behind the bushes and took him back in the Micra."

Even though we'd begun to walk uphill, my legs were light with relief.

"So you weren't involved, Ritch?"

"Only a bit – otherwise, well – you know."

"Yeah, I understand. It was good of you to look after Tanner."

"Yeah, well. He's a mate."

"I like Tanner," I said.

Moor Park is huge. I heard it said once it was the second-largest park in England. There's a bowling green, a golf course, a boating lake, a children's zoo, and even then, in the middle, there's a vast expanse of grass. From the top you can get an amazing view of our town. That was where we seemed to be heading. It's funny how the higher you get, the smaller your problems seem. Perhaps because people look tinier, and their concerns are tinier.

We sat down on a bench at the highest point.

"Look, Ritchie, I don't think we ought to have any more to do with Loz and Woodsy."

"Why not?"

I was surprised he had to ask. "Well, they didn't stick to the plan. And if we're a gang, then you've got to obey orders."

"But the plan collapsed when Tanner was ill."

"Yeah, but we made it clear at the meeting that we're doing what we do without hurting people if we can help it, and targeting people who deserve to be hit, and helping the needy!"

"Sure, but sometimes someone's going to get hurt. That's the world we live in."

"Ritchie, no. Someone vandalised Donna's car – it was an old Mini and she can't afford to get it fixed."

"That's tough," he said.

"And Loz is racist."

"A lot of people are."

"But it's wrong!" I could hear myself pleading. I sort of wanted to argue with Ritchie but at the same time I couldn't bear to. That's why there was this strange whining note in my voice.

"Look, I'm not defending what they did, Anna. But they got jumpy, sitting in the Micra for so long. It was, like, bound to happen."

"So you're saying, we've got to accept that not everything will work out the way we want it to? There's bound to be mistakes?" I was struggling to understand.

"That's right." He smiled at me. I was encouraged.

"It's like collateral damage!"

"You what?"

"Collateral damage," I repeated. "You know, in war, when the army bombs civilians by mistake, or fires on friendly aircraft."

"You're clever, you," Ritchie said approvingly. "That's exactly what it's like. Brainy Anna." He dug me in the ribs.

What I like about Ritchie is that he respects me, see. Some boys are put off if girls come across as clever.

"I'm still gutted for Donna," I said. "And I'm not sure Woodsy was right about Mr Singh."

"Forget them now, Anna," he said, and that was when he kissed me. A kiss tasting of the cold outside air, of cigarettes, of Ritchie. I gave myself entirely to it.

He said afterwards, "They didn't get us. The cops, I mean."

"Yeah," I said, nestling against him.

"Nothing and no one can get us."

It certainly felt like that, sitting on the bench overlooking Moor Park. Beneath us was a dark blur of trees hiding the boating lake from view. You could just about see the main road, and further in the distance were the tower blocks of Fairfield, and hundreds and hundreds of rooftops. Only we mattered.

"You've got to be one step ahead, you see," Ritchie said. "If you use your brains, you won't get caught. You've got to have nerve, too. Nerve is important."

I was only half listening to him. I was content just tuning in to the rise and fall of his voice. As I did, I was thinking how happy I was at this particular moment in time, alone with Ritchie, the past successfully behind us, the future what we would make it. The consciousness that Ritchie cared for me – that I had a boyfriend – just overwhelmed me. I could have cried from happiness.

"We're not like the others," Ritchie said.

"So we can just drop them?"

"Not entirely. We need Loz. Well, his brother. Did you know his brother was a squaddie?"

"I don't know much about your mates," I said, just enjoying the sound of his voice.

"There's not much to know. Loz lives with his brother. He moved in with him after he came back from Bosnia – he lifted loads of stuff while he was there – he's a right criminal. You see, Loz's mum ran off with some bloke and went abroad. When he was five. He was in care for a time but then when his brother shacked up with this bird, they took him in. Then she walked. I don't know who's living there now."

"What about Woodsy?" I asked.

"He lives with his gran and his dad. His gran can't get out of the flat because of her arthritis. His dad's a lazy bugger, can't be arsed to do much else except watch the box with a few cans, know what I mean? Woodsy stays round at Loz's, most nights. What else? Tanner you know about."

Tanner was bullied and beaten up till he was unconscious. That was a year after his mum died. I knew he lived with his aunt and cousin. It was all pretty depressing. When you think about it, it was hardly surprising lads like that went off the rails. I decided not to blame them. And then there was Ritchie himself. His life hadn't exactly been a bed of roses either.

It was as if he was reading my mind. "Me and Wendy – we're going to see him tonight."

"Your dad?"

"That bloke, yeah."

"What – I mean, does he know…?"

"No. Wendy's been watching him. She knows he leaves the office around six thirty. We're going up there and she's going to have a word."

I wasn't sure what to say, so I just asked simple questions.

"Where's his office?"

"On the Calder Fields Industrial Estate."

"Are you scared?"

Ritchie shrugged. "Not scared. But sometimes I feel as if I could... Anna, I know. Let's go taxing afterwards."

The word thrilled me. I caught my breath.

"Yeah. Why not?"

"Why not?" he echoed me.

We moved off the bench together, almost racing down the hill. Then I had an idea. "Ritchie," I said. "You know something. My mum's away this weekend."

"Is she?"

"Yeah. Why don't you come over to mine?"

"I might just do that."

"Bet you can't catch me!" I cried as I ran off from him. Ever since I was a kid I've loved running downhill. I can run pretty fast. I dodged between the trees, confident Ritchie would run after me. Then out on to the path again. Running, running. And then into the children's playground, not caring what people were thinking, dodging through the swings. And into the bushes. That was where he caught me, grabbed me from behind, and I struggled but he was stronger than me and he pushed me down on to the ground. I protested I'd get dirty. We rolled around together for a bit and I wondered if he was going to kiss me. He didn't. He just seemed to want to pin me down, and for a moment I was frightened. I could feel the suppressed violence in the hands that held me down. What was happening here? My heart was pounding. I struggled out of his grip, got up and brushed the leaves off us. Ritchie just laughed. Normality was restored. I looked down at myself. Luckily I wasn't in too bad a state.

I checked my watch. It was already six.

"Shouldn't you be meeting your mum?" I asked. I showed Ritchie the time.

"Yeah," he said.

"I'll come with you. Then we can go off after that. I'll wait at the top of the estate. I'll be OK."

The truth was, I wanted to be there for Ritchie. I thought this meeting might be difficult for him. I hoped his mum wouldn't mind.

Ritchie was still for a moment, considering my offer. Then he said, "Let's go."

CHAPTER FOURTEEN

When we got off the bus, Wendy was there, in jeans and an old sheepskin jacket. She didn't react at all to my presence. I realised then I didn't matter to her. She was so focused on her meeting with Ritchie's dad, that I was at worst an irrelevance and at best a witness.

"He hasn't left yet," she told us. "I've been watching the road."

There was only one, one-way road going through the industrial estate, near the centre of town. It looped round and all the various businesses and offices were sited along it – modern, anonymous buildings. The bus stop was by the exit road. We turned into it and followed Wendy, who walked ahead of us with determined steps. Ritchie didn't say anything to me, and I couldn't think of anything to say to him. He seemed kind of tense, and I guessed he just wished the whole thing was over. If it was me – if I was about to meet the dad who disowned me when I was a baby, I'd feel a mixture of things – I'd be angry, and anxious, but also I think I'd want him to like me – to see me and suddenly realise what he'd been missing. Maybe Ritchie felt those things, but if he did, he wasn't going to say.

Eventually we came to a large builders' yard, with a

glass-fronted office looking out over it. There was the BMW in the car park. On the wall above it, the words *Peter Duff* were painted in white. The lights were out in the office reception. All was quiet. A slight breeze disturbed some dust on the ground. I could see the yard in the distance. It was full of piles of bricks, sacks of cement, other builder's stuff.

"Here's something interesting," Wendy muttered to Ritchie. "You know Sandra, who used to clean at the pub? She's working for him now – in his home at Burnham. That's a coincidence, isn't it? It must mean something. It's fate."

Ritchie made some comment I didn't catch. We were standing just by the exit from the car park. If Ritchie's dad came out of the office, we'd be able to confront him in an instant. Wendy opened her handbag and took a packet of cigarettes out and handed one to Ritchie. They both smoked in silence.

Meanwhile I was feeling more and more as if I shouldn't have come. When Ritchie was with his mum he was different. It was like he only existed in relation to her. He moved and spoke like she did. He smoked in the same way as her. It was like they were tied together by an invisible cord. I wished I was somewhere else. But to go now would be disruptive and disloyal. I knew I had to see this out, even though it wasn't my story. At least, it wasn't then.

Suddenly Wendy clutched Ritchie's arm. In the same instant I noticed a figure come out of a side door and into the office. A large, burly man in a suit. He stood by a desk and checked some papers. I felt my pulse racing.

"It's him," Wendy said.

Ritchie stubbed his cigarette out. I tried to back off a little. Then the office door opened and the man turned to lock it. As he did so, Wendy walked into the car park. Ritchie stayed with me. We couldn't quite hear what happened. But I saw everything.

He turned, caught sight of Wendy and flinched in surprise, maybe even terror. He was a big man, receding hair, jowly face, but most definitely Ritchie's dad. The eyes were the same. Wendy was talking to him intently. He was standing stock-still. I could tell he wanted to get away but couldn't see how to. Then he decided to make for his car. Wendy followed him and got between him and the driver's door.

"Craig!" she called.

Ritchie left me then and went over to his mum. I didn't know whether I should follow him or not. But I did anyway. The truth was, I wanted to see what was going to happen. I *had* to see what was going to happen.

"Craig," Wendy said. "This is your father."

Peter's eyes locked on to his son's, and in that moment I knew he'd acknowledged him. A shiver went through me. I could see fear in his face, fear and confusion.

"I'm not asking for much," Wendy said, breaking in. "I just want to hear you say Craig is yours, and treat him as you do your other kids. Give him the things you give them. Look at him, Pete, look at him. Your own flesh and blood. Admit it. Pete, look at me. Remember what we used to have, Pete."

She scared me more than ever, Ritchie's mum. You could tell she'd rehearsed all this. She was so intense, you felt drawn into her world. But there was something pathetic about her too. She reminded me of those women you get on Oprah or Jerry Springer, living so intensely in their own dramas they don't see how ridiculous they're being.

It's quite easy to see what people are thinking by looking at their faces. I saw Peter look at Wendy with something like disgust. When he looked at Ritchie, he was bothered. But Ritchie's face was unreadable, even to me.

"This is harassment," Peter said. "If you don't go away, I'll call the police."

"I dare you," Wendy said. She put a hand on his arm. He pushed it roughly away. I could hear my heart thudding in my chest. I hoped there wasn't going to be violence.

"Leave her alone!" Ritchie shouted.

It was turning ugly. I knew it would. I held my breath.

"Craig – keep out of this," Wendy said. "Peter, listen to me. You can't turn your back on the past. You know how you felt about me. We're your real family. But I don't want a lot from you. I just want you to look after your son. Tell him – tell him you're his father. Tell him you'll support him. Do it."

Peter's face was like a mask now. I could tell he'd had time to think, to collect himself. He wasn't going to give in. Whatever feelings Ritchie had roused in him had been totally extinguished. He spoke to his son now, as if he was a stranger, or like he was an apprentice in his yard or something. "Be a good lad and take your mum home. If you don't, you'll give me no option but to call for the police."

Ritchie's dad shot me a sidelong glance. At that moment I thought that adults are such hypocrites. They're always telling us to be honest and confront things and work hard and keep to the straight and narrow, but here was this man being such a louse.

Ritchie's face was white with anger. In the nick of time Wendy placed a restraining hand on him. "He's not worth it, Craig. Don't get yourself into trouble. Peter, you haven't heard the last of us. We'll be back. You know you can't get rid of me that easily."

Peter took his mobile out of his jacket pocket and began to dial a number.

"You coward!" she taunted him. "You're frightened of me and two kids?"

Peter spoke into his phone. "Mike? Sadiq? I'm having a spot of bother here. Yeah, in the yard. If you could come over." Then he disconnected.

"Mr Big can't fight his own battles!" Wendy laughed at him. "Come on, Craig. There's no point hanging around now. There'll be other opportunities."

She turned on her heel and Ritchie followed her. We three marched out of the car park and along the road. Then Ritchie stopped by a wall. He hunched over and began to retch. I felt so sorry for him. But he was OK. He wasn't sick or anything. Finally he collected himself, only he was white as a ghost. Wendy hadn't noticed him stop at all. She was ahead of us, muttering to herself.

When we got to the main road I noticed Wendy's cheeks were flushed and her eyes were glittering. "Shall we go for a drink?" she asked us.

Ritchie said, no. He told her he was going to take me home. She was so wrapped up in herself she didn't seem to mind. So they said goodbye. Ritch pulled me roughly along the street. He was full of a sort of pent-up fury, and he scared me. I turned to see his mum lighting another cigarette. Soon we were at the bus stop.

"Do you want to talk?" I asked him. I thought it might be a good idea if he off-loaded to me.

"No point," he said. "No fucking point. Let's go taxing."

"Are you sure you—"

"I said, let's go taxing."

Just then the bus came into view. I thought maybe it was for the best – Ritchie needed to distract himself. He needed time to come to terms with what had happened. And nothing takes your mind off all your problems like taxing does.

Soon we were on the bus, on our way to our next heist.

When we arrived at Princes Street, the upmarket end of the town centre, the streetlights were on and it was night proper. Ritchie said Princes Street was where the money was, and that's where he wanted to be tonight. Me too – I love going out at night – the lights, the buzz, the dark alleyways, all those people, all those different lives. We were where the action was. We strolled up and down, past all the restaurants and wine bars. Pizza Express, J D Wetherspoons, Café Rouge, Bar 38. All these chains, all on the make. Lots of people all dressed up to the nines, self-consciously enjoying themselves. I got glimpses of people perusing menus, waiters carrying half-eaten meals away – I mean, it's obscene, don't you think, the way people play with food when there's famine in Africa and places? I saw women posing, throwing their heads back, laughing. Men talking to impress each other, leaning across the table, gesticulating. Young men, middle-aged men – I thought, I bet this is where Ritchie's dad goes out to eat. We watched them all, all those people, knocking back their drinks, getting out of their heads. They thought they didn't have a care in the world. Little did they know that we had the upper hand. We were in charge here.

We went into Dunne Street, where there were some pretty swanky pubs and clubs. There was a notorious, exclusive membership-only club where a very well known celeb was caught with a prostitute. I asked Ritchie, if it was so exclusive, how come she got a membership? A bouncer stood outside it.

I was beginning to wonder what Ritchie had in mind. On the bus, we hadn't made any definite plans. I watched him casing each joint, his eyes scanning the territory, looking for something. I realised then that part of what I loved about him was exactly that – I *didn't* know what he was thinking. He was unpredictable. He made me live on the edge, and the edge was the best place to be. It was like walking along a precipice – you needed every iota of nerve, every bit you possessed. I wondered how long we could go on for. I didn't want it to end, but I guessed one day it would. I fought a feeling of bleakness that threatened to swamp me. I wanted to savour every moment of tonight. And it turned out to be our best night ever.

We turned into the next street, past a basement Italian restaurant and a couple more bars. I noticed a silver BMW sports car. I pointed it out to Ritchie. It had one of those irritating personalised numberplates. This one read DAN 4711. Then I saw something else.

"Bastard," I said. He's parked in a disabled spot. I bet he's not disabled!"

OK, so I know you can be rich and a cripple, but still! We walked over to the car and I looked for an orange disc, the sort with the clock where you set it at the time you arrived. Nothing. There was nothing in the car, either, to show the driver or a passenger was disabled. On the back seat was a pashmina and a bag from Bank, sealed at the top. These guys had just been shopping.

"Doesn't it make you sick, Ritchie?" I said.

He didn't reply. He didn't hear me. He was on the other side of the road. I was puzzled. I crossed over and asked him what was up. He hushed me and pulled me away. Once we reached the corner of the street he said, "Look at the couple sitting at the table in the bar with the red window frames. You'll see the bloke keeps looking at the BMW."

We wandered past on the other side of the road. Because it was dark outside and the restaurant was well lit, it was easy to see the diners. I immediately picked out the couple Ritch had been talking about. Table by the window, steel bucket with a bottle of champagne sticking out the top, two huge wine glasses, blonde bimbo type of female who kept shoving her hair behind her ears, bloke yakking on, boring her, most probably. And, yeah, he kept eyeing the car. There was no doubt in my mind at all that the car was his. He was checking for traffic wardens.

When we got past, Ritchie said, "The second he sees a warden, he'll be out there, pleading innocence. Or offering them a bung."

"So what are we going to do about it?" I challenged him, sick with excitement.

"Are you sure you're up for it?" he smiled.

"Just try me."

We were getting cold after fifteen minutes of just ambling up and down the street, but every time we passed the restaurant, just as Ritchie told me, I remembered more and more of the layout of the restaurant entrance, and perfected my part of the plan.

Just when I thought the moment would never come, the woman got up, picked up her tiny handbag, and went to the ladies. There were no waiters about. I went and stood just by the restaurant door, where I could see what was going on. Ritchie entered.

I didn't hear what he said to the bloke, but it didn't matter – I knew what he was saying anyway. He was asking the bloke, "Is that your BMW? Because, I thought you might like to know, there are some traffic wardens round the corner. And a towing lorry."

The bloke shot up out of his seat and fumbled in his jacket pocket for his car keys. Ritchie watched him, then followed him out. Exactly at that moment I attempted to enter the restaurant, partly blocking them.

"Excuse me," I said. "I'm looking for Chez Nicole's and none of these restaurants have got their names outside. I've got to pick up my sister."

"No," said the bloke, annoyed and flustered. "It's Coco's."

"Ooh, sorry," I said, gormlessly. I timed it so I turned to leave the restaurant at exactly the same moment as the bloke, squeezing through the door, accidentally jostling him, apologising again. But he was so stressed about his motor, he ignored me. Then I walked off left and back on to Dunne Street. I heard the sound of a car revving up and being driven off.

"Come on!" said Ritchie, appearing by my side, panting heavily. "But don't run!"

We walked off swiftly, purposefully. In a moment we were back on Princes Street. And our luck was in. A bus arrived at the bus stop and we didn't even check where it was going, just jumped on, paid our fare and went upstairs.

Ritchie took it out of his pocket: a brown leather wallet, old and thick with promise. He opened it. There were twenties, tens, some change. Loads of cards, scraps of paper, sales receipts. I didn't know what to say so I made a fairly obvious comment.

"The cards won't be much use."

"No," Ritchie said. "He'll cancel them as soon as he realises his wallet's gone."

"Which will be when he tries to pay the bill."

I could just imagine it. He reaches into his pocket, looks everywhere for his wallet, tries to explain to the waiter, realises it was probably us who nicked it, because he remembers being jostled, but it's too late. Maybe the girl has to pay. Then they go out to his car—

And then, as I saw the car in my mind's eye, I said, "Ritchie? Where's the nearest hole in the wall machine? You know – a bank machine." I could hardly get the words out, I was so excited. Ritchie looked along the road.

"We'll get off at the next stop ," he said.

We did, and sure enough, there was a NatWest.

"Give me the debit card. I want to try something."

Ritchie handed the card over. I inserted it in the machine. It vanished from sight. Then the on-screen instructions said, *Enter your PIN number.*

I keyed in, 4711.

Select which service you require, the machine said. I pressed cash, no receipt. £200. *Please wait for your cash*, we were told. We waited. Out slid the card, followed by the notes. I counted them and gave half to Ritchie.

"Anna," he said. "You're amazing."

When I got home that night, I took an envelope from the drawer in the kitchen where my mum keeps our stationery. I put my hundred pounds in there, and stuck a stamp in the right-hand corner. Then, writing with my left hand, I addressed the envelope to Mrs Singh at the hospice. I kept it under my pillow overnight and in the morning, on the way to school, I posted it in the letter box at the end of our street.

CHAPTER FIFTEEN

I checked myself in the mirror again. I thought the blusher looked a bit too obvious, so I rubbed it off. I pulled my black trousers a little lower – yeah, just right. The top I was wearing was one of those off-the-shoulder ones. It was also black, but with a kind of silver thread in it. I put some glitter gel on my shoulders. Karen lent it to me when I told her my boyfriend was coming over for dinner.

I checked my watch. Still a quarter of an hour before he'd said he'd arrive. I was ready far too early. Even the food was almost ready, not that I was doing anything that fancy. Just a spaghetti bolognaise – I'm used to making that as I do it for me and Mum quite a lot. Some ice cream for afters. Ritchie said he would bring some booze.

I'd made an effort with the table. I got all the candles from my bedroom, that people had given me as presents, and a couple of Mum's aromatherapy ones, put two of them on the table, and dotted the rest about all over the place. I put some R&B on the music system. I mean, was I sophisticated! The candles were a good idea, as their flickering light made the living room look different, not like the place I shared with my mum.

Mum knew that I'd invited Ritchie over for dinner. It was amusing watching her reaction. She was going on about, I'm glad you won't be alone, and it's nice to have a tête-à-tête.

"A *what*?" I asked her.

"A tête-à-tête," she answered. "It's French. It literally means head to head. Two people alone together."

"Head to head sounds more like a fight!" I exclaimed.

"Well, let's hope there won't be any fighting," she said. "Or any of the opposite of fighting."

"The opposite of fighting?" I questioned, though I knew exactly what she meant.

"You're only sixteen," she said. "Take it easy. Don't do anything you might regret."

"I'm not a fool," I told her.

"I don't want him staying the night."

"I know, I know."

We were both pleased when that bit of the conversation ended. I told her to have a brilliant weekend and not to worry about me.

Five minutes to go. What if he didn't turn up? How would I survive the disappointment? It amused me to think I was so nervous, just as nervous as when we went out taxing. There was one difference – now I didn't feel in control. I went into the kitchen to check the bolognaise sauce. This was Ritchie's idea, this meal. I'd just said to him, come over at eight. And he'd said, what's on the menu? I thought he was joking, but he *wanted* us to eat together.

And just at eight, the bell gave its throaty buzz, I took a deep breath, made my way out to the hall, and opened the front door.

For a moment I didn't recognise him. Here was another Ritchie. He was wearing a jacket and tie. I tried to hide my surprise. And he was carrying a bunch of flowers and a bottle of something. Well, I say I tried to hide my surprise. Actually, I failed. I started to laugh, and went, "Look at you!" But the self-consciousness I saw in his eyes stopped me in my tracks. "Look at you!" I said. "You look gorgeous!" I gave him a brief kiss on the cheek and he came inside. He looked around the house and I remembered this was his first visit here.

"It's nice," he said.

Now that was odd. Our house is OK, don't get me wrong, but it isn't the sort of place you'd comment on. But Ritchie was kind of interested in it. Isn't it funny, you think you know someone pretty well, and then they do something that makes you reassess them. Ritchie was tough, why should he be interested in a *house*? But he was. He walked around, looking at the furniture, the paintings on the wall, our knick-knacks. I even felt a little jealous.

Then I thought, he's only acting. He's treating this like we were going out taxing. We were role-playing again. As soon as I realised this, I felt better, more at ease. I could join in. So I said, "You wait there. I've got to check the pasta."

"I'll pour us a drink. Have you got a corkscrew?" he asked.

I felt all giggly. "Sure!" I went and fetched one, and carefully he opened the bottle of wine he'd brought. It looked posh – it had a French label. He poured me some and I only took the tiniest amount.

"Mmm," I said. "I can detect roses… and haystacks… and petrol fumes!"

He grinned at me, and drank his.

It wasn't too long before we were seated at the table with the spaghetti I'd made. Ritchie seemed really hungry – at least he dug in with gusto. He said it was good, and I felt a little splutter of pleasure at that. I discovered I wasn't too hungry though. It was the strangeness of the whole situation. I thought I'd better carry on with the role-play.

"Had a nice day at the office, dear?" I joked.

Ritchie just smiled at me.

"I've put the children to bed," I said.

"You're nuts," he replied.

I felt uneasy again. Why wasn't he joining in? I tried a bit more pasta. Nope – I wasn't hungry.

"You're a good cook," Ritchie said. "I can cook too. So that's something we can share. One day."

"Sure," I said.

"Do you and your mum eat together?"

"Most evenings," I replied. "Unless she's working late."

"I think families should eat together," he said. "It's good for the kids. It helps bring them up properly. Do you want some more wine?"

I didn't, but I forced myself to drink some. I thought it might help. Maybe I was wrong, inviting Ritchie over. Maybe our relationship worked best out on the streets. We ate in silence for a bit. As we did, my mood changed again. I kept stealing little glances at him. Ritchie. My boyfriend. My partner – in crime. In my house.

"One day we might have a place of our own," he said. "Then we can do this most nights, like a normal couple. And we'll be loaded then. We'll have a proper entertainment centre, one of those flat-screen TVs and a DVD player, and watch films. Cos I'm gonna have a good job, me. I might be an actor. Yeah, I'd go to college, then drama school, then audition for parts. So we'd need to move to London, Anna. You could still see your mum. She could stay with us. Cos we're gonna have this huge house, with spare rooms and that. And a garage. With three cars."

"Three?"

"Yeah, three. In case one breaks down. And you'll go to college too, as you're dead brainy."

All of that felt scary and exciting to me at the same time. I felt as if I couldn't breathe. I was so happy that Ritch saw his future with me, but robbed also of my voice in it. It was weird, thinking of us as respectable. But the idea had its appeal. Maybe the taxing was a stage we had to go through, to prove ourselves to each other. But the future would be different, on the level. I decided to test him.

I asked, "And will we still go taxing?"

"No way. We won't need to. We'll just have a laugh about what we used to do."

"Yeah," I said, losing the thread a little. The wine and the food had made me feel sleepy. I thought that I didn't want to be on the other side of the table to Ritchie any more, as lovely as he was to look at. I wanted to be next to him. So I kicked him under the table, as a sort of suggestion.

"What do you want?" he asked.

"Nothing."

The CD that was playing came to an end. I got up to put another one on, and as I was passing Ritchie he put his hand out and stopped me. Next thing, I found myself on his lap, and we were kissing.

It was seriously weird kissing like that, at the dining table. I pulled him over to the sofa. And soon I forgot where I was. I was back in that dark, unexplored territory of our bodies. And we didn't even need a new CD. We needed nothing.

I guess you're curious about what happened then, whether we ended up in my bed or not. It's OK, I don't mind talking about that stuff. I'm not embarrassed. In fact, it's even kind of relevant. We did go up to my room, and I'd decided that if Ritchie wanted to go the whole way, I would. If he had a condom with him, that was. You see, I never wanted to say "no" to Ritchie, ever. But the funny thing was, nothing like that happened. He asked if he could stay the night, and of course I said he could. We got into bed together, and hugged, but he didn't try anything. It didn't matter. Being so close to him, all tangled up like that, was one of the best feelings I'd ever had in my life. The sex bit wasn't very important.

But it kills me, the way everyone makes out that blokes are only after one thing, and here's Ritchie, Public Enemy Number One, reluctant to force himself on me. Or maybe he didn't feel like it. Then I began to wonder, why? Was there something wrong with me? A crazy idea, but once it had planted itself in my head like a tiny seed, it grew and grew until it was all I could think of.

So we lay in my bed, side by side, arms round each other, and I said, "Are you OK?"

"Yeah," he mumbled.

"I kind of thought, you might want to... you know."

"Do you?"

"I don't know," I said.

"Pass me over my fags," he said. I did. They were in his jeans pocket. He lit up and I thought I'd better get rid of the smoke before my mum gets back. Ritchie took a huge drag on his cigarette, then sat up in the bed. The duvet fell away, exposing his bare chest. He's quite skinny, Ritchie. You could see the faint outline of his ribs.

"Have you got an ashtray?"

I looked around and passed him an old jar that used to have face cream in it.

Then I said one of those stupid girlie things I thought would never pass my lips. "Have you gone off me?" I asked him. "Don't you fancy me any more?"

"Of course I fancy you," he said, quick, determined, as if I was daft to ask (which I was). "But there's stuff on my mind."

"You mean with your dad and everything."

He nodded, took another drag. I was kind of pleased he'd brought this up. We hadn't spoken about that weird episode at the builders' yard, although I'd thought of it a lot. I'd wondered what Ritchie was going through, and what he was going to do next. I was about to find out.

"Wendy says that was the last straw for her – seeing him disown me. She said all the feelings she had for him died, when he did that. She *says* that, but she still goes on about him. This mate of hers that cleans for him, she keeps going out with her and finding stuff out. It's like the more she knows about him, the more it gives her power over him."

"Yeah. I can understand that."

"But me, right, I don't bloody care if I never see him again. The bastard, the..." He came out with a string of expressions you wouldn't want to hear. For a minute, he looked like his mum, haunted and rage-filled, eyes dark with fire. "If that was me, if I'd brought someone into the world, I wouldn't just cut them out of my life. He's a coward, he's scum. Worse than scum."

"So are you going to cut him out of *your* life?" I asked, hoping the answer would be yes.

"He's my dad," Ritchie said, and as he stubbed his fag out in my face-cream jar, he looked young, like a kid sitting up in bed, waiting for someone to come in and kiss him goodnight. Then his face hardened again. "He owes me, Anna."

I nodded. I agreed with him. You can't deny your own flesh and blood.

"So I'm gonna take what's mine. Wendy doesn't know this. But I reckon that will shut her up, too, if I put things right. Like when we tax, Anna. We're putting things right – making the rich cough up for the poor. So I'm taxing him. And when I've done that, and Wendy sees, she'll drop the whole thing."

"I'm sorry – I don't understand. What do you mean? How are you going to tax him?"

"We'll get into his house and nick some stuff."

I could feel my heart pounding. This was dangerous, this was way out of our league. Very casually, I asked, "How are you going to get into his house?"

"I've thought about this. You see, this mate of my mum's – she's his cleaner – she has keys to his house in Burnham. I could get copies made. So we could get in and just help ourselves. He's rolling in it, Anna. That BMW – that's one of *three* cars he owns. His kids go to private school. His wife doesn't work, she doesn't need to clean at the pub, coming home smelling of fag ends and stale beer. So we'll get in there, you and me, and help ourselves."

"No," I said.

He looked at me quizzically. But that "no" had slipped out before I even knew I was going to say it. Once I'd said it, I knew I was right. "Drop it, Ritch," I said. "Just drop it. I know he's scum but I... but I think we'll get into trouble." I sounded pathetic. Ritchie thought so too.

"Getting into trouble hasn't bothered you before."

"I know, but this is different. He knows you. He'll guess it's us. It doesn't feel right."

"I don't care if he knows it's us," Ritchie said. "That's the point. And he'll be so ashamed he won't grass on us. We'll get away with it."

I shook my head.

Then Ritchie looked at me, long and hard, and turned his head. Just turned it. And I felt him withdraw from me to somewhere unreachable, until it didn't even seem as if he was sitting up in my bed at all. I could sense the bond between us unravelling. I thought, what would happen if this was the end? If my refusal to work with him means he drops me? I felt cold and empty inside.

"Look, Ritchie, it's just that I think it's a bad idea."

"I talked to Loz about it. He said he'd help. He gave me... some advice."

I was jealous of Loz. I liked him the least of Ritchie's mates. "Don't take Loz. He's bad news."

"He's my mate," Ritchie said.

"If I came with you, would you leave Loz out of it?"

He turned his face back to me and smiled. It was like the sun coming out. "Yeah," he said. He took my hand and held it tight.

My mind raced. I thought, if I went with him, I could keep an eye on things. I could look after Ritchie, check he didn't get into trouble, maybe even persuade him to change his mind at the last minute. He needed me there. He couldn't be trusted in his dad's house, not alone, certainly. Thinking about it, I had no option. I didn't, did I? If it was you, you would have done the same. You'd have stuck by Ritchie. Because I reckoned

I was probably the only sane person in his life. He needed me. It felt good to be needed. But I had one more thing to say.

"Just make me a promise, Ritchie."

"Yeah?"

"This really will be our last job ever."

"It will be," he said.

"Because after the trouble at the golf club, I didn't feel good, Ritchie. The wrong people got hurt. I want to stop it, stop taxing."

"So do I." Then he reached out and stroked my hair. He said. "I love you, Anna."

"I love you too," I replied.

"And all I want is for us to have a normal life, and just be together, and after all this, we will. Just you and me. And I'll come here and you can introduce me to your mum. And we'll just go and see films and stuff, and we can go to college. We'll have a life, a proper life."

I nodded furiously.

"Just one more job," he said. "Our last one. Ever."

CHAPTER SIXTEEN

And so, fast-forward to the next Friday – it's hard to believe all this happened just a few weeks ago. But like I said, I had a bad feeling about what Ritchie wanted to do, right from when he first mentioned it at my house until that Friday morning, when I was walking down St Edward's Close. It's a new estate in Burnham. I can remember them building it. All the houses have double garages and the further down the cul-de-sac you get, the larger the houses become.

I had to remind myself why I had agreed to come in on this. It was only because I thought Ritchie needed me. I even had the idea that once we had got inside I could dissuade him from taking anything, and we could go away with our hands clean and start afresh. Our hands clean. That's funny. I was dressed as a cleaner. I chose some cheap jeans specially and I borrowed a sweater from Mum. I thought cleaners dressed like that. I don't really know as we've never had a cleaner.

Maybe the bad feelings came from the fact I didn't sleep much the night before. I was tossing and turning and having those dreams when you actually think you're awake and then something bizarre happens, and you still think it's real. Even when you wake up you still think it could have happened, and you have to work out bit by bit that you dreamed it.

But I'm going off the subject. I was heading for Number Thirteen. Thirteen, St Edward's Close. It turned out to be right at the end of the street, a brand-new house built of honey-coloured bricks with white paintwork. It was massive. A semi-circular flight of steps led up to the front door. But I knew to go round the side, as that was the way the cleaner came in every other day.

Ritchie and I had been through this over and over again. In my pocket I had a copy of the keys. Ritchie was vague about how he'd got them, but it was through this friend of his mum's. Apparently Wendy knew nothing about it. I also had the digits 2387 etched in my brain – that was the security code for the burglar alarm. I was to let myself in, making out as if I was the regular cleaner. Once inside, I was to turn the radio on in the kitchen as that was what the normal cleaner always did.

It was lucky it was half term and Mum was back at work. Obviously this was a job we had to do on a weekday. Then once I was in, I would have to wait until Ritchie arrived in a van he'd borrowed from Woodsy's dad. He would pretend to deliver a big box of something; I was to let him in, and we were going to fill it with stuff. Ritchie was going to take it back to the van and drive off. I was to wait a little longer, then let myself out. It sounded simple, and the more we went over it, the more foolproof it seemed.

But I still had bad feelings, although I tried to hide them from Ritchie. The truth was, I just couldn't summon up the enthusiasm I used to have for taxing. It had gone sour on me. Maybe I'd taxed just to get close to Ritchie, and now he was mine, I didn't need to do it any more. Or maybe... that time when we taxed the bloke with the BMW, that felt final to me – as if *that* should have been the last time. Today felt wrong, as if we were pushing our luck. But please don't think I'd changed overnight, and had become a goody-goody. It was more that my appetite for crime had gone. It had sickened and almost died. I made my way round the side of the house and stood there for a moment, summoning my nerve. The ordinariness of the morning struck me. The sky was blue but cloud-flecked, a plane droned above me, all was normal. I tried to pretend I was just a new cleaner, going to do my first job of the day. But it was no use. A black band of pain gripped my temple. The effort was almost too much for me.

I tried the keys in the glass-panelled side door. In a moment I had unlocked it, and stepped into the kitchen. An insistent tone reminded me to see to the alarm. I found the panel and keyed in the numbers, then looked around me. I swore under my breath. It was magnificent. The kitchen was huge, with a free-standing cooking range in the middle. There were more units and stuff all around the perimeter, a marbled work surface and a breakfast bar with trendy little black leather stools. It was like the sort of kitchen you'd see in a magazine. The window over the sink gave a view of a huge garden with a swimming pool, covered over now. The sheer opulence of it affected me. If this all belonged to the man who'd ruined Ritchie's life, then it didn't seem fair. If he had the front to deny his own son, then there *was* some justice in our coming in and taking things.

I remembered to look for the radio. I noticed a small TV and video player. (I thought we could take them – old habits die hard.) I saw a couple of empty wine bottles standing on a partly open dishwasher. I guessed it might be the cleaner's job to switch it on. I located the radio – a digital radio – and played around with it until I got Funk FM. It was the "Something Old, Something New" hour. They played something contemporary and then a cheesy oldie.

And now what? It occurred to me that while I was waiting I could actually do some cleaning, but I didn't feel like it. It was odd, standing there in somebody else's house without an invitation. I took off my anorak and scarf, putting them over one of the stools. I left my gloves on – Ritchie's instructions.

Well, I couldn't just stand there like a lemon, so I made my way out of the kitchen to have a look around the rest of the house. I came out into the hallway. Amazing. It was like one of those houses in the movies. The hall was big enough to be a room all by itself. A door to my right was open and revealed a massive living room, and on one wall was a huge flat-screen TV like a mini-cinema. To my left was a smaller living room, with toys scattered around it, and the dining room kitted out with a long table and tall chairs with curvy backs.

But what really got me were the stairs. They actually came down in the centre of the hall. The upstairs rooms were along a sort of gallery, with an ornamental balustrade. The staircase curved round at the bottom, echoing the shape of the staircase outside the house. I tried to imagine what it would be like, sweeping down that staircase. I didn't know people actually *lived* like that.

I made my way up the stairs, and when I got to the top, I looked down. From the kitchen I could hear that old song, *Lady in Red*. I tried to imagine myself in a red ball gown, or one of those slinky dresses that hug your hips but have a train at the back. So I slowly made my way back down the staircase, shimmying just a little. I imagined Ritchie waiting below to meet me, in a tuxedo, a bunch of flowers in his hand. He would whisk me off somewhere dead romantic.

In my dreams. Because Ritch and I were just a couple of thieves. The thought was an uncomfortable one. Again I wished I was out of there. Or just that Ritchie would hurry up. I stood in the hall, willing Ritchie to ring at the door. He was going to give two short rings and then a long one. All was silent. I was far too nervous, too jumpy to keep still. Adrenaline forced me to keep moving.

I wandered into the little living room, where the toys were. This was cosier, on a more intimate scale. There was a TV in here too, a cabinet full of ornaments, and I made a mental note that some of those would be worth a bob or two. Also, on the windowsill, was a row of framed photos. Since the window was only at the side of the house, I imagined I'd be safe going over to take a closer look.

I picked one up. This was Ritchie's dad, Peter, but dressed for a posh dinner, in a penguin suit. He was grinning, his hand on the shoulder of the woman in the picture with him – his wife. She wasn't unlike Ritchie's mum, Wendy. She was also blonde, thin, fragile-looking, but there the resemblance ended. She looked like she'd stepped off the pages of a magazine. Her make-up was immaculate, her dress screamed money, she looked preserved by her wealth, as if she'd bought eternal youth. I wondered how much of it was plastic surgery.

The next picture was more informal. Here was Peter again, sitting on a long leather sofa. Snuggled up to him was a girl who looked about ten, hair in a high ponytail, clutching a Barbie doll. Next to her was a little boy, scruffy blond hair, cheeky grin. Ritchie's half-brother. The lucky one. He had a look of Ritchie about him, but you could tell he was pampered. And there they all were again in the next picture, on some foreign-looking beach, mum in an embarrassingly tiny bikini, kids building a sandcastle, yachts moored in the distance. Then I thought of Ritchie and the flat he shared with his mum.

Now, you're thinking that I was beginning to come round to Ritchie's point of view, that this crime was justified. But somehow the pictures had the opposite effect. Yes, it was all totally unfair. Ritchie was cheated. I felt more sorry for him than I can say. But I couldn't see how what we were going to do would make things any better. Rather than proving he deserved better, by robbing his dad Ritchie was going to prove he was as worthless as his father thought.

I jumped out of my skin as there was a thump and a pile of letters landed on the mat inside the door. I found myself retching with fear. I hadn't realised till that point quite how scared I was. I took lots of deep breaths to calm myself. I heard the manic voice of the Funk FM DJ from the kitchen. I picked up the letters to put them on the table by the door. I looked at them. Most were for Mr Duff, some to his wife. A couple looked like birthday cards.

My hands were hot inside my gloves: red woollen gloves that were one of last year's Christmas presents. More than anything I wanted to take them off and wash my hands. I noticed a cloakroom off the hall and thought I would probably be safe going in there, turning on the taps with my gloved hands, waiting until the water was running nice and hot, then taking off my gloves and washing thoroughly. It would be a relief to feel the water running through my fingers, taking away the heat of fear and panic, cleansing me, purifying me. As I moved towards the cloakroom I thought I heard the doorbell ring. It was hard to tell over the music. So I darted back into the kitchen and saw someone's outline against the frosted glass. As I got closer I could see that it was Ritchie.

The first thing I noticed about him when I opened the door was that he'd had his head shaved again. And that he was wearing a huge grey-green parka with a hood. Also that he was carrying a large box and had a holdall dangling from one arm. He looked for all the world like someone delivering a TV. He took the box into the kitchen and I shut the door.

"Why have you had your head shaved again?" I asked. Daft question, but it was all I could think of to say.

"I just felt like it," he said. He put the box down by the door and I watched his eyes stray across the room. I knew he was thinking what I was thinking earlier. Here was serious money. I followed him out into the hall to the strains of a Dido song.

"Ritch," I said. "What are we going to do now?"

"Look around. Take what we want."

"We could just look around, and then go. It's not too late to change our minds." My voice was urgent.

Ritch wasn't looking at me. He seemed paler than usual. He shivered in his parka. Maybe he had the same bad feelings I did. I hoped so.

"Let's go," I said.

"No." It was definite, final.

I went to put my hand on his arm, and when I did, I could feel his arm tense like steel. "Leave me alone," he said.

I had a problem here. Ritchie was already so worked up I didn't think he would listen to me. My instinct told me confrontation would be the worst thing right now. Instead I thought I'd normalise things, lighten up. Then maybe he would come to his senses.

"This is some place," I said.

"It makes me sick," he replied.

"I know. That he should be so wealthy, after what you told me. I didn't realise builders could become so wealthy. Did he build the house?"

Ritchie wasn't listening. He left me and went to look in the living room. I saw him focus on the pool outside the French windows. Having had his fill of that, he moved back into the hall. He began to climb the stairs. I followed him, not letting him out of my sight. Once on the landing we both saw a huge painting of Ritchie's dad with that woman. Next to it was the master bedroom. A king-size bed was unmade, a pale pink bedspread lying on the floor. An elaborate dressing table was loaded with bottles and brushes. Ritchie walked over to it and picked up a small box, which looked like it contained jewellery. I thought he was going to put it in his pocket, but instead he lifted it as if to throw it.

"No! Don't!" I screamed. He stopped and regarded me. "Because if you cause damage, you'll leave clues. Just take what you want and we'll go. Please."

Ritchie sat down on the bed and looked around. I wondered why he wasn't in more of a hurry. Usually when we taxed we were as quick as lightning. I was getting more and more nervous. Then the bedside phone began to ring. We both jumped. It trilled a couple of times, then a gruff voice said, "If you want to leave a message for Pete or Janice, speak after the tone." Then the caller put the phone down.

"Let's start," I urged. "I want to get out of here. It spooks me."

"Soon," he said. "Look. There's a bathroom through there?"

"Yeah. An en-suite. They've left it in a mess."

Ritchie began to fiddle with the bedside radio. It was set to Classic FM. A piano concerto was playing.

"Ritchie! Take something and go, for goodness sake!"

"Sshhhh," he said.

I was thinking, he's crazy, wanting to listen to music at a time like this. But then I could hear what he had heard. A door banging. A man's voice.

"Janice?"

I was paralysed with fear. Then I wanted to run, but couldn't think where to run to. I glanced at Ritchie. He was listening attentively, then slowly got to his feet.

"Janice?" went the voice. A gruff voice I recognised immediately as Pete's. "Where are you? Are you OK?"

My skin was icy with terror. We would be caught red-handed. Could I pretend I really was the cleaner? I might just get away with it, except for the presence of Ritchie. And why had Pete come back? Either this was a terrible coincidence, or – God forbid – Ritchie had planned it. He could have left a message at his dad's work, saying Pete had to come home, Janice wasn't well, or something like that.

Footsteps. "Janice?" More footsteps, ascending the stairs, becoming louder. I could not think of one plausible thing to say. Ritchie had his hands in the pockets of his parka. Pete came into view then, and walked through the doorway. His face was a picture of astonishment and terror.

I turned to look at Ritchie, seeking guidance.

And then I saw the gun in his hand, pointing directly at his father.

CHAPTER SEVENTEEN

I couldn't take my eyes off the gun. It was metallic with a black trigger. Ritchie's hand only shook slightly as he held it pointed towards his dad. I'd never seen a real gun before. I wondered how Ritchie had got hold of it, and then remembered Loz, and his brother who'd been in the army.

"Shut the door, Anna," Ritchie said.

I did because I thought the best thing for now would be to play along with him. And although half of me was shocked rigid, the other half could not believe that Ritchie would actually shoot that thing. He must have felt uneasy about having it as he hadn't mentioned it to me. I had to walk round his father to get to the door, and I could have run for it, but I wouldn't leave Ritchie. I returned to where I was before, in front of a half-open wardrobe. Ritchie was standing by the head of the bed, facing his father. And apart from Ritch telling me to close the door, no one had spoken a word.

I was trying to piece together what was going on here. If Ritchie had lured his father back to the house, then he never intended to rob him at all. If he came with a gun, then his plan was to... My mind shied away from the inevitable conclusion. He was going to shoot his dad. No! Those kind of things only happened in films, in gangsta lyrics. Ritch and I taxed, sure, but we never harmed anyone. He never harmed anyone. Then I remembered how he tried to mug me in town all those weeks ago, and I went cold. I thought I knew Ritchie. I thought I loved him. Only there wasn't time to reflect on any of that now. At any moment, that gun might go off.

I looked at Ritchie's dad's face. It's funny how you can tell someone is more terrified than they have ever been in their life, and yet there are hardly any signs. He wasn't screaming, he said nothing, in fact, but he was drawn and deadly pale. I noticed then that Ritchie's hand – the one that had the gun – was trembling more than ever. Ritchie sat down on the bed, but he still had the barrel of the gun trained on his dad.

"Don't try to get away," Ritchie said. "If you move, I'll shoot."

His voice trembled, and I think that gave his dad courage. He put out a hand to the wall to steady himself, and swallowed before he spoke.

"Craig? Please."

Ritchie had his eyes and the gun locked on to his father. Maybe, I hoped, all he wanted to do was frighten his dad. Or get him to agree to give him money. Yeah, that would be it. This was only a sort of blackmail attempt, or getting money by extortion – it *was* taxing, of a sort.

Still no one said a word. An impassioned female voice began an aria in a foreign language. I wondered if I should turn the radio off.

Then Ritchie spoke: "Admit it. Tell me to my face that I'm your son."

"You're my son," came Pete's voice. But they were just words, spoken by fear and not by the man. Ritchie knew that.

"You ruined Wendy's life. You owe us."

"Tell me how much you want. I'll give Wendy a cheque."

Ritchie glanced at me as if he was consulting me. "Say an amount, Ritch. Then put down the gun," I whispered.

"Ten thousand pounds," Ritchie said.

That seemed like a lot of money to me. But maybe to Pete it was nothing. I hoped he'd have the sense to agree to Ritchie's demands.

"OK," Pete said. "Send Wendy to my office tomorrow. But give me the gun."

I knew Ritchie wasn't going to do that. But I was beginning to feel hopeful. I could see that we could escape from this. If Ritch stood up now and, with the gun pointed at his dad, left the room, me with him... Then Ritchie made an error of judgement. I know why he did this. You see, really it wasn't the money he wanted at all.

"Tell me why you left us," he said. "I need to know. What's your version?"

I knew what he wanted because I'd been there too. When my dad left my mum, what was so awful was that it felt like he was leaving *me*. I thought he didn't love me – if he did, he'd have stayed with us. But my mum was brilliant. As messy as it all was, and even though her heart was breaking, she explained to me over and over again how my dad still loved me. And he said so too. Deep down, I knew they were telling the truth. But Ritchie – from his point of view, his dad walked out on him, and wouldn't even acknowledge him. Where his self-respect was, there was a big black hole. Self-respect – that was what he wanted from his dad now, and it was too late to get it.

"Put the gun down and I'll tell you." Pete was sounding a little more confident now. That note of authority was creeping back into his voice. Here was a man who believed in himself, one who was used to ordering others around.

It seemed to have an effect on Ritchie. To my exquisite relief, he carefully placed the gun beside him on the bed, close to his leg.

"We weren't suited, your mum and me," Pete said. He was gabbling – it was hard to catch his words. "She's a strong woman, always wanted her own way. She gave as good as she got. I'm not saying I didn't raise a hand to her, but she threw a pot at me..." He glanced at the gun. "Like mother, like son," he murmured. Ritch heard that and he placed his hand around the trigger. Pete didn't seem to notice.

"She always had to go one better. I'm not saying I didn't have other women – we were never married, me and Wendy. But what she did, when she found out, she went out on the town and didn't come home for three days. I heard all sorts of stories. I took her back, but only for a while."

As he was speaking, justifying himself, wiping saliva from the side of his mouth, I felt Ritchie's hatred for him. Pete relaxed. He was so convinced of the truth of what he was saying, he didn't see that Ritchie might not feel good about this.

"You see, lad, I'll pay the ten thou. I know how you feel. But in all fairness, I'm pretty sure you aren't my son. The fact is, you could have had one of several fathers. Your mother was no angel. She put you up to this, did she?"

He should have never said that. I knew Ritchie would explode at this insult to his mother. That was why I reckoned it was up to me to take some action. I could tell Ritchie was so keyed up I couldn't just lunge at him and get the gun. He'd fire it, and that would be that. Instead I moved over to him and put my hand – my gloved hand – on his shoulder.

It was too late. Ritch gave a cry that was something between a yelp and a sob, and jumped to his feet. Once again the gun was trained on his dad.

I knew without a shadow of doubt that he was about to fire.

What happens at times like that, is that you move quickly but your brain stays calm and logical, so there is a slow motion effect. I thought, *I must stop Ritchie getting into any more trouble*. Next I thought, *He wouldn't shoot* me. So I threw myself at his dad and clung to him.

"Anna! What the fuck are you doing?"

"Put the gun down!" I screamed.

I couldn't see what was happening. My face was pressed against his dad's shirt front. I felt the heat of his chest, smelt the sour stink of fear, heard his heart racing. My eyes were screwed shut. Then I heard the crack of a bullet. I thought, quite calmly, *I'm going to die*. I never imagined this would be my death. I felt utterly detached, curious. Then a split second later there was a deafening explosion of glass. The dressing-table mirror was smashed into a thousand pieces. Ritchie had shot his dad's reflection. I remember the smell – like fireworks. I turned. Glass was everywhere. His dad's image was shattered.

There was a small part of me, tucked away deep inside, that was terrified. Yes, there was a red, pulsing terror somewhere in my body. But my mind was clear. It was as if someone was speaking to me, giving me instructions. This voice said, *Get the gun from him, Anna*. So I left his dad, and said softly to Ritchie, "Give me the gun." And he did.

I said to his dad, "Don't tell anyone about what happened today. Because he's your son, and you know it. You can do that much for him." The man nodded. Do you know, that scared me more, the fact that I could make an adult do what I wanted. I didn't like that feeling. I was going off the whole power-trip thing.

"Come on, Ritch," I said. Together we left the room and walked downstairs. I was still totally calm, so much so that I remembered to get my things from the kitchen. The radio was still playing. We left by the side door. I followed Ritchie to a rusty white van with the word *Fellowes* on the side. I noticed his dad made no attempt to follow us.

Once we were on the road, wave after wave of fear and panic washed through me. I felt sick and tried to stop myself retching. The van picked up speed.

"Ritchie!" I screamed. "Slow down!"

But he paid no attention. The van tilted precariously as we rounded a corner.

"You'll kill us!" I said. Then, after a pause, "Where are we going?"

"I don't know," he said. "And I don't care."

"Look." I was desperate with fear. "Let's go to my mum's surgery. No – we need to get rid of the gun. Whose is it, anyway?"

"Loz's brother's." So I'd sussed one thing out correctly.

"Shall we drop it off there?"

"They're all out."

"Ritchie, it's really serious to be in possession of a gun. You'll be put in jail."

He didn't respond. He swerved round a corner and on to a road leading north. It wasn't going to be easy to get him to stop. I could imagine only too well what was going through his head. He'd planned this macho act of revenge, and it had failed. He was lower in his own estimation than he ever had been. Not only that, but whereas before he'd had one parent he could believe in, now his so-called dad had robbed him of her, too.

All Ritchie had left was me. And what a mate I was! If it wasn't for me leading him on to tax, it was doubtful whether he'd have cooked up this foolish scheme. I'd let him think it was all right to take the law into our own hands. But it wasn't – I could see that now. There has to be limits, for our sakes, as well as everyone else's.

And there we were, speeding down the dual carriageway, really speeding, way over the limit, the two of us in a borrowed car, Ritchie without a licence, still breaking rules and this time, risking our lives. We were idiots – we had been idiots – and we were going to die like idiots.

"Ritchie – slow down!" I screamed.

But then it happened. We were approaching some traffic lights and they turned to amber. Ritch put his foot down but they had still turned to red before we got there. We shot across the junction.

"Ritchie!" I remonstrated. Then I saw, waiting at the lights at the crossroads, a police car. We were right in its line of vision. It pulled away sharply and turned the corner to pursue us. The sirens blared and lights flashed.

"Pull over!" I screamed.

But it was no use. Ritchie just picked up speed. The road we were on led out of town. It was wide without being a dual carriageway, and not too busy. We were going faster and faster.

"They'll catch us in the end," I shouted. "Pull over now! Now! Now!!"

It made no difference. Then I realised something. Ritchie wasn't trying to escape from the police. There was no way he could escape. He was bent on self-destruction. He couldn't cope with the whole situation, and oblivion seemed the only answer. So, yeah, I was terrified, more terrified than I'd ever been in my life. But now I saw how I could stop him.

"Ritchie," I shouted. "I'm scared! You're going to *kill* me!"

It worked. He jammed his foot on the brake. I felt that van slow, and then skid. He lost control, you see. But he lost control because he was trying to save my life. When I saw the lamppost, I thought it would stop us safely. I was glad we weren't going into a wall.

I'm sorry, that's where my memory ends.

CHAPTER EIGHTEEN

The mind does that, doesn't it? Really bad stuff gets wiped out, so you don't remember it. The next thing was that I was waking up in hospital with my mum at my bedside. She's been wonderful, my mum. You'd have thought having to deal with me would have brought back all her depression, but it's almost been the opposite. She's been busy fighting on my behalf. She's amazing.

But you know all about that. You were there on the panel that decided what to do with me, after I'd made a clean breast of everything. You heard how she said, and how the head at school said, I was of previously good character. He also started to say I'd been led astray, until I interrupted and gave him what for. The truth is, I still think I corrupted Ritchie. A bit like Lady Macbeth. Or maybe it was his mum who was like Lady Macbeth. Whatever.

So then you came into my life, my probation officer. I thought you'd be like some sort of prison-warder character, but you're not. You've been more like a good mate. Which is why I've told you all this, every little bit of it. And I also told you because you said you'll be there when Ritchie comes out of hospital, when he goes in front of the panel. You said you'd make sure he gets the best outcome. He never meant to kill his dad, just frighten him. That's what he told me afterwards. I know there's a risk of a custodial sentence because of the gun – listen to me! *I* can talk the talk now. *Custodial sentence.* Wouldn't it be funny if I ended up doing law – me, the ex-criminal. Because I am an ex-criminal now. I've learnt there's never a good reason for a bad crime.

I keep thinking what happened when I went to visit Ritchie in the hospital. I was out of there in twenty-four hours as I was only shocked and bruised. It wasn't really a miracle. My seat belt saved me.

Ritchie wasn't wearing his. That's why I nearly lost it when I saw him, lying there with all those tubes and drips. He'd smashed some ribs and ruptured his spleen. His face will be badly scarred. Did you know, they don't wipe the blood off your face, the nurses? That gave me a shock. When I first saw him, part of me just wanted to run. But then I thought, *Come on, Anna. You can get through this.* But it really got to me, seeing Ritchie smashed and useless in the hospital bed. Anyway, he was only concussed, not in a coma or anything. I was able to sit with him and hold his hand for ages. I was sitting there and thinking that he was in such a mess on the outside, but the mess inside was probably worse. He'd smashed himself up completely.

His whole life was in pieces. I know it will take him time to reassemble them. He might come out quite different. I'm going to have to get to know him all over again.

He might not want to see me, I'm aware of that. I might remind him of a time he wants to forget. I also know I might not feel the same way about him. But I owe it to both of us to find out. Did I tell you my mum went to visit his mum? She's been in touch with various people, and Ritchie's mum is getting help – medical help, I mean. So when he comes out of hospital he can live with her to begin with. My mum's also said that Ritchie's dad has vanished from our area, but that's good, as he hasn't pressed any charges.

The funny thing is, I thought we were clever, doing what we did, outwitting everyone. I had us down as brave, streetwise, smarter than your average. But the real test of our courage starts now. Owning up and starting over is the hardest thing of all.

But I'm up for it.

DISCONNECTED

SHERRY**ASHWORTH**

"It's hard to know where to begin. I'm not even sure who I want to talk to. Or what I want to say. But maybe if I try to put all the different parts together it will make some sort of sense. So here's my story, and it's for each of you to whom I owe an explanation. But remember, I'm not sorry."

Catherine Margaret Holmes
Loving and dutiful daughter.

Cathy Holmes
A-level, A-grade student.

Cath Holmes
Friend and confidante.

Cat
Risk taker, thrill seeker, rebel.

Will that do as an introduction?

0-00-712045-1
HarperCollins*Children'sBooks*
www.harpercollinschildrensbooks.co.uk

BLINDED BY THE LIGHT

SHERRY**ASHWORTH**

*At first glance they looked dead ordinary.
A few blokes, a girl in a white dress, faces
you might see anywhere. But on closer
examination they did look different. And
then it dawned on me. Everyone seemed
remarkably happy.*

When eighteen-year-old Joe meets Kate
and Nick on the train, something about
them appeals to him. He goes to see
them at their commune, and gradually,
his life starts to make sense. With the
White Ones his life has a purpose. So he
decides to leave his family and live with
the White Ones for ever. But there is
something sinister afoot...

0-00-712336-1
HarperCollins*Children'sBooks*
www.harpercollinschildrensbooks.co.uk